DOCTOR WHO

The Glamour Chase

The DOCTOR WHO series from BBC Books

DOCTOR WHO

The Glamour Chase

GARY RUSSELL

BOOKS

1 3 5 7 9 10 8 6 4 2

Published in 2011 by BBC Books, an imprint of Ebury Publishing.
A Random House Group Company

ISBN 9781849903158

Mixed Sources

Product group from well-managed
forests and other controlled sources
www.fsc.org   Cert no. TT-COC-2139
© 1996 Forest Stewardship Council

FSC

Commissioning editor: Albert DePetrillo
Series consultant: Justin Richards
Project editor: Steve Tribe
Cover design: Lee Binding © Woodlands Books Ltd, 2010
Production: Rebecca Jones

Printed and bound in Great Britain by
CPI Cox & Wyman, Reading, RG1 8EX

To buy books by your favourite authors and register for offers,
visit www.rbooks.co.uk

For Eòghann Renfroe

Once upon a time, a long way away, the TARDIS whooshed and zoomed and spiralled through the space-time vortex. To one of the occupants, this was the most exciting, thrilling and fantastic thing she had ever experienced. And basically, she guessed, it would stay that way for the rest of her life.

And she had met the man who flew this amazing, extraordinary and fantabulous ship only a couple of days before. He had arrived on her home planet and saved it from a massive… thing that was rotting its very core away. The actual soul of the planet was dying, and he stopped it. Repaired it. Saved billions of people, all by himself. Just one man in a blue box. He wore odd clothes, had strange hair and spoke in a weird way. He asked for nothing in return, just some company for a few hours with her family, and they made him dinner and washed his jacket, which had got a bit manky during his heroic manoeuvres.

And so they had offered him a reward, to thank him. They offered him the Glamour, but he didn't know what they meant, so they tried to explain, and began demonstrating it to him. But he said no anyway.

And they had accepted his decision, even though they didn't understand it, because they could see there was a sadness in him. He had an aura of dislocation, of homesickness. Of recent farewells. Yet he was polite but adamant, and he told them stories of his travels, of his adventures. Of his friends and enemies. He told them of the universe and its 700 Wonders. Of Federations and Alliances, Empires and dictatorships. And they told him of their enemies and friends, of their star system, its planets and moons. Eventually, after a lovely evening watching the moons rise above the now-safe horizon, he had said it was time to go.

And the others in the family and friends who had shared food begged him to stay. To accept the award he was due, the recognition by a grateful planet for what he had done to save them all. But he had said no. Said that he didn't want applause and plaques and trinkets with inscriptions on. He was satisfied that he had helped a people in need, stopped a planet and its occupants going extinct.

And, he added, he'd had a great meal, and that

really was the best 'thank you' he could have had.

And he had set off for his odd blue box, his jacket washed and pressed, and she had run after him, not wanting him to leave.

And he had explained, gesticulating up into the sky, pointing out stars and moons and planets and galaxies, that his life was out there. And his friends. And his enemies. And he had to go and see someone about a planet or a starship or a space station that needed his help just as her world had done.

And she had pushed past him as he was unlocking his blue door, squeezed between his long legs and rushed in, expecting to find herself in a small dark box.

And instead she was in a wonderland of thrills and marvels.

And it didn't even occur to her at first that it was bigger on the inside than the outside; she was so dazzled by the light, the warmth, the feeling of life – albeit alien life – that permeated this huge room with its indented walls and the strange device in the middle with all the switches and levers and dials.

And he had smiled at her and asked what she was doing, and she had gabbled about how fantastic it had to be out there, in space, and one day she would be out in space too. And he'd said that was a great dream to have and to give him a call when she was out there and he'd pop by and say hello, because his blue box travelled in time as well as space. And she didn't doubt that for a minute, because if he could fit all this inside a tiny blue box, then travelling in time couldn't possibly be difficult.

And she had told him that she'd be old enough to travel in about fifteen years, and he gave her a small green sphere and said to use it when she wanted to find him, and he'd come and say hello.

And she had wondered if he wouldn't be terribly old by then and retired and at home with his friends and a family, feet up in front of a fire, with a cup of herbal brew, reading books and suchlike. But he had laughed, saying that was unlikely: he could travel in time, so fifteen years for her might be five minutes for him, and he was getting quite good at flying his ship to specific points these days and did she want a quick spin?

And she had said yes, and so he had closed the door and got her a small box to stand on so she could reach the edge of the central device thing whatever it was with the switches and levers and dials, and she held on tightly. The Doctor winked at her, rubbed his hands together and yanked a rod down, and the blue box that wasn't either a box or blue inside made a huge noise, wheezing and groaning, and the central column thing in the middle of the device she was gripping on to started going up and down. She wanted to block out the sound, but at the same time she wanted to embrace it all and love it and enjoy it and adore it, because she knew this would not last for ever.

And, seconds later, he had opened a huge screen

and she could see space and all those planets and stars and galaxies he had talked about. He took her beyond the moon, down the space-time vortex corridor, across a nebula, and into a writhing cloud of jades and purples and golds and silvers, which, he said, was a new star system being born.

And then he took her home. He opened the door of his blue box and said he'd look forward to hearing from her.

And she grasped the little green ball he'd given her firmly in the palm of her small hand and swore to herself that she'd never let go of it. She smiled, because she knew that she would see him again. One day.

And he was gone. His blue box faded away, amidst that awful but beautiful noise. She stared up at the stars for a moment and then ran back to her family, deciding not to tell them where she had been (unless hours had passed, then that would be difficult). But it turned out only to be minutes, so she kept quiet.

And lived her life exactly as she wanted to.

Chapter
1

'**Commander, we are losing** hull integrity, and shields are down to forty-eight per cent.'

The Commander nodded, without looking up from her console. 'Thank you, 3. Are the crew in stasis?'

3 consulted his screen, just as it started to short out. 'I think so, ma'am.'

A small automatic fire extinguisher emerged and squirted fire-resistant liquid over the console. Then it failed.

3 casually reached out and absorbed the fire extinguisher, allowing it to deconstruct and simultaneously nourish his own body. One of his earlier scalds immediately healed. 'How much of the ship can we safely take on ourselves?' he asked the

ship's Medic, who was stood by the bridge entrance, scared beyond belief.

'It's nearly all gone,' he stammered. 'Just creating the stasis chambers took most of the living areas. The galley's gone too.'

'Damn,' said the Commander. 'And I wanted a snack.'

3 grinned at her. 'I wish 3715 were awake to hear you say that, ma'am. He'd be overjoyed that you actually wanted to eat his food.'

The ship shuddered.

'We've entered a new system, Commander,' said the Navigator from her console.

3 looked at her – barely out of the Ball, and her first mission would most likely see her death. He crossed over and stood behind her, noticing for the first time a massive gash across her left shoulder.

'You OK?'

'I'm good, sir.' She tried a brave smile, but he wasn't fooled.

'No you're not.' He threw a look back at the Medic who was just staring at the panoramic view screen showing the new star system ahead, as if staring at that – at some fixed point – would stop his nausea. No time for that now. 'Medic, attend to 456915 please.'

No reply.

'107863!' he snapped. 'Do your damned job!'

The Medic reacted as if slapped and hurried over to the Navigator.

The Commander threw her Exec Officer a look. 'He's scared, 3. We all are.'

3 nodded. 'I know, ma'am.'

The Commander sighed and started tapping commands into her black-box recorder. 'Let's jettison this and hope it finds its way home.'

'From out here, ma'am, that could take centuries,' said the Tactical Officer to her right.

3 shrugged. 'Procedure must be followed.' He nodded at the Commander. 'I'll take it to the exhaust pods, ma'am, when you are ready.'

The Commander looked at her bridge crew. What was left of it, after the stasis chambers had claimed the rest. 'Listen, people,' she said. 'No matter what happens, we all get into stasis, is that understood?' She looked 3 straight in the eye. 'No heroics, 3, understood? We lived as a team, we sleep as a team, is that understood?'

3 nodded.

With a deep breath, the Commander activated her recorder.

'This is Commander 128 of the WSS *Exalted*. We have temporarily evaded the Tahnn ships that were pursuing us and have sought refuge in a solar system my Tactical Officer refers to as AK Apple Dot Point Oblique. He also refers to it as primitive, inhospitable and with a sun giving off far too much radiation, but then 25463 would. He's like that.'

She winked at the grizzled Tactical Officer beside her.

'As I record this, my crew are in stasis and I am preparing to reassign the interior contours of the ship to the external structure and go into cocoon mode. Only myself, EO 3, TO 25463, MO 107863, SC 6011 and NO 456915 remain conscious. If you can follow this recorder back to our ship and rescue us, we'd be grateful to say the least. If not, it's been a fun ride and I hope when you get this the Tahnn are but a memory that once blighted our society and world. This is Commander 128 signing off.'

The Commander stabbed the controls and the tiny soft black box rolled out. She scooped it up and passed it to her Executive Officer. 'We'll see you at the stasis chambers in five minutes.'

He nodded and left the bridge, hearing one final command from 128.

'That planet there, the atmosphere is breathable at least. Bury us there!'

And the door closed behind him.

As he walked through the corridors, he reached out with his left arm and felt the interior walls flow into him and then straight back out into the outer walls, creating a thicker cocoon skin. Chairs, consoles, discarded chess sets, everything briefly drew into his body and then back out again, preparing the ship for its fiery descent into the planet's atmosphere.

One area didn't accede to his command to dissolve, which meant it was still occupied. He tapped the comms outside the door. 'Counsellor?'

'On my way, sir,' was the Counsellor's voice from within. 'I'm just sending out my own records of the crew.'

The door slid open and, as it did so, it melded into the walls and began fading, being drawn into the body of the Counsellor who stood facing 3.

'Your records could be appended to the Commander's,' 3 said.

The Counsellor didn't agree. 'Even though it probably won't make it home, it's my duty to keep my notes and records of the crew separate from Command's.'

3 nodded. He understood that; the Medic on the bridge would probably have done the same.

Together they marched forwards through the empty corridors, the Counsellor's quarters now completely gone. They reached the exhaust tubes and as the ship shot past a small satellite above a red planet. 3 pressed eject and the small recorder shot back out on its trajectory to home.

It would take a long time to get there. And that was assuming the Tahnn, not known for adherence to intergalactic treaties, didn't intercept or vaporise it first.

3 and the Counsellor faced an interior wall. 3 absorbed it then spread it behind him, conjoining it to the exhaust tube, which similarly melded itself into the outer wall of the ship.

The massive area ahead of them had been sixty rooms on eight storeys. All that structure was now lining the hull, and the cocoon was nearly finished. Once the Commander led the evacuation of the bridge, she and the Tactical Officer would absorb everything there and spread it around the nosecone for added protection.

As the Counsellor wandered to their assigned stasis chamber, a far wall faded away to reveal the crewmembers from the bridge.

'Reporting for duty,' 3 joked drily to his Commander.

Medic 107863 put the Counsellor, the Navigator and then the Tactical Officer to sleep first then shrugged. 'One of us has to be last,' he muttered. 'Might as well be me. It is, after all, my job.'

The Commander touched his cheek. 'You will have five seconds to put yourself in stasis afterwards. Are you sure you want to do that? 3 and I are trained for that kind of speed.'

The Medic shook his head. 'You and the Exec are also far more important to the crew afterwards.'

'Not true,' 3 retorted. 'We might need patching up. You don't need a miserable git like me. Get in, Commander. You too, 107863.'

The Commander watched as the Medic sighed and got into his chamber. The door grew around him and, with a hiss, he was asleep like all the others.

'Just you and me, 3' said the Commander. She kissed him on the cheek. 'Good luck, my friend.'

3 allowed himself just the tiniest of smiles. 'This ship, this crew – best in the fleet, ma'am. We don't

need luck, the Tahnn do. When we are recovered and the ship has had a chance to re-knit, we'll be back out there, leading the fleet to victory. In the meantime, ma'am, as last officer standing, I'm ordering you to get some stasis-induced sleep, cos I know what you're like if you've not had enough sleep. Ma'am,' he added with a wink.

Wordlessly, Commander 128 placed herself in the stasis chamber, which wrapped around her and closed. A second later, she was unconscious.

3 gave his now empty ship a last look around, feeling the buffeting as they entered the atmosphere of the third planet of this little-known system.

He only had to activate the controls, reabsorb them and throw himself into his chamber.

All in five seconds. Or he wouldn't sleep, and just die in agony.

Nice.

Taking a final breath, he kissed the palm of his hand and touched the floor of the ship. 'Thank you,' he said. 'You've looked after us well.' Then he straightened up, slammed a hand on the control.

His stasis chamber began to open for him, and he quickly absorbed the control console then all but hurled himself into the chamber – it was already starting to close.

'Five seconds my—' he grunted out loud. 'More like three…'

The chamber cocooned around him, and he was asleep.

So neither 3, his Commander nor anyone else on the WSS *Exalted* felt the ship crash down through the atmosphere, skimming and bouncing on the air currents, veering across mountaintops and over oceans until it reached the area selected by Tactical Officer 25463 as the safest place to land.

To bury itself deep beneath soft earth.

And there, the ship would repair itself while its crew slept.

Well, that was the plan, anyway...

Wulf and his son Owain had a job to do. Or two jobs, really. The first was to stand on the hill and look out to the great waters beyond and light fires if they saw boats approaching. The second was to herd the goats that supplied their village with food and milk. Wulf and Owain took both jobs very seriously.

When the Sky Gods threw a huge dark object from the skies towards them, they really had no idea what to do. So they both dropped to their knees and prayed to the Sky Gods that this wasn't some kind of retribution.

The noise the object made as it ploughed into the fields beyond the village was louder than anything Wulf had ever heard before and he screamed as he covered his ears.

Then it stopped.

He opened his eyes, seeing his fellow villagers flood from their huts, shooing goats and dogs from the area, the womenfolk keeping the children back whilst Village Elder Tor led his strongmen towards the crashed object. Tor reached out to touch it but pulled his hand back, burnt.

Wulf could hear his cries of pain and fury from atop the hill. He told Owain to stay with the herd and dashed down to his fellow men below.

'It is from the Sky Gods,' he yelled. 'It has to be.'

Tor nodded. 'But what should we do?'

For three days, the men guarded the object and talked at length about it. About what it meant. About whether the Sky Gods were angry or whether it was a gift.

In the end, Tor made a decision.

Over the next month, using the most rudimentary shovels and axes, they performed a technological miracle. They dug beneath it so it slowly sank further into the ground, and then they erected a wooden protective shell around the exposed top half. They buried that under earth meticulously carried up from the coast where it was damper and therefore softer.

And Tor, Wulf and the others lived their lives, safe from invaders, with healthy wives and children and goats.

After a few hundred years, the contents of the mound were forgotten. Stories and myths built up around it. It was a god. It was a warrior chieftain. It was a sacred rock from the stars.

It stayed that way, a mystery for over four

thousand years. Until, in 1936, Mrs Enola Porter, an amateur archaeologist living in Norfolk, rammed her shovel through the mud and into the outer hull of the WSS *Exalted*.

The world would never be quite the same again.

Chapter

2

It was a hot summer's day in Little Cadthorpe.

The sky had that glorious blue you believe only really happened when you were a child – when it reappears, and proves it really does exist, you can't help but be happier than usual. That amazingly strong sun that could be felt on the skin and the lack of clouds just added to the joy that was today: 14 August 1928.

The depression in the city was in decline and, although his family had lost much, Oliver Marks (Regimental Sgt Major, retired) was happy. His strong hand was firmly gripped around Daisy Conlan's. Or, as she had just agreed to become next spring, Daisy Marks.

'I love you, Miss Conlan.' He grinned, pushing

aside a low-hanging tree branch that threatened to impede her walk through the woods.

She smiled back. 'And I, Olly, adore you.' She looked behind them, suddenly concerned. 'But Olly, where are Davey and Calleagh?'

Oliver frowned. 'Who?'

'Why, Mr Marks, have you forgotten our children so quickly?'

Oliver laughed. 'Ha! So, just two children is it? And Calleagh? What kind of name is that?'

Daisy stopped and wagged a finger at him. 'I will have you know, sir, that Calleagh is a good Celtic name. I had a Great Aunt called Calleagh, back in the old country.'

Oliver feigned pensiveness for a moment before walking on. 'I fear, Miss Conlan, that I could not marry a fibber. I know your family quite well and, even when exploring the darkest ends of the Giant's Causeway, I have never come across a relative of yours called Calleagh. Alas, alack, our engagement is at an end, if you insist on naming our future offspring after imaginary matriarchs.'

Daisy scampered after him, now looping her arm around his and pulling him closer. She kissed him on the cheek. 'Truth is… No, never mind.'

'My dear, I shall cease conversing with you forthwith if you do not halt your prattle.'

Daisy laughed. 'Ooh, listen to you with your big words. I did know a Calleagh who I was very deeply in love with in Ireland, and it is also a name I adore and want our daughter to be named.'

'Who was she?' Oliver asked, a twinkle in his eye. 'I genuinely don't remember ever hearing your father mention her. He, as you can imagine, gave me chapter and verse on the Conlan family back to the 1600s!'

Daisy took a breath. 'Promise you won't laugh or be cross?'

'Oh, I shall enjoy this explanation,' Oliver said.

'Calleagh was a puppy I once had. A most beautiful chocolate brown one with lovely big, pleading eyes and a pink tongue and—'

'And you expect me to agree to naming our daughter after a dog?' Oliver roared with laughter. 'I cannot wait till she is 18 and you have to explain that to her, because I most certainly shall not.' He kissed her quickly on the lips. 'But it is a wonderful name, so I shall endeavour to ignore the dog connotations and believe there really was a fearsome Great Aunt about whom your father omitted to tell me.'

Daisy looked at him, giving his arm a squeeze to make him stop walking, and ran a hand through her auburn hair. 'I really do love you, Oliver,' she said. 'Thank you for asking me to marry you.'

He smiled back at her, cupping the back of her hand with his hands. 'As I recall, it was in fact you, with all your emancipation and Emmeline Pankhurst attitude, who asked me!'

Daisy nodded. 'Well, I asked you to ask me. And why not, you silly sausage. It's not as if you were going to get round to it otherwise, were you?'

'I thought you'd think marriage was some antediluvian concept for oppressing women,' he said. 'Curiously, I take your beliefs and opinions very seriously, Daisy Conlan.'

She sighed. 'God, I love you so much,' she said, and kissed him. 'I wish we didn't have to wait until March.'

'Weddings are expensive,' Oliver said, 'and I know your father well enough to be certain that he'll want to put on the biggest and best wedding he can for his only daughter. And, with the state of the world's finances at the moment, he'll end up laying off some of the lads just to make ends meet if we try to marry this year. And that is something I won't have on my conscience at any cost.'

Daisy understood.

She and Oliver had met at a rally in London four years previously. He'd survived the Great War and, in doing so, had reshaped his views and allegiances drastically. He had campaigned for the Labour Party and not for the Conservatives, as his family always had. This had cost Oliver a lot: his father had all but disowned him, and many of his fellow officers had stopped talking to him. But she had been drawn to his dedication, his firm belief that so many young lives had been lost or shattered during the War due to politics. So many of the upper class had become officers, leading good, solid men during battles with no actual experience or knowledge of warfare; they held their ranks purely because of who they were, or how much money their families had.

Oliver was kicking against that – he said rank should be progressive and not a product of elitism. If some of the men in the trenches had been made lieutenants or captains instead of people with no field experience whatsoever, how many thousands of lives might not have fallen under German bullets and shells? Truth was, thought Daisy, no one would ever know. But she admired – no, *loved* – his passion on the subject and his deeply held belief that the 'common man' deserved respect, equality and the chance for power.

She had been at the rally to support women, who had seen their place in society rise during the War. So many good strong women working in factories, in hospitals, on the buses and trams, in the farms and schools. Women doing jobs that ten years earlier, only men would have been considered fit for. And yet, when the War ended, they had soon found themselves facing an attitude best summed up as 'Yes, thank you, now go back to breeding children, darning socks and making tea for the menfolk at work'.

Women had come on in leaps and bounds since then – the vote had been such an important stride forward. But there were still those in the Government who sought to squash those achievements, reverse those policies. Daisy had seen an opportunity to move to London, become embroiled in the London

Set and work from within to keep things moving forward for women, and not back to some dark Victorian age. She had even met and spoken to Lady Astor on the subject, which was a personal achievement, she felt.

Her reverie was broken by a whining noise from… above. It was no aeroplane, she was sure of that. Oliver had heard it too, and he was already shielding his eyes against the sun and trying to look to the heavens.

'The trees are blocking the view,' he said, waving his hands towards the canopy. 'Let's get out into the open.'

They hurried out of the copse and onto the village green. Sure enough, half a dozen other groups of people were there, all looking up, trying to discern the source of the noise.

Oliver felt a blast of heat directly above him. He looked around, trying to trace its source, but could see no sign.

'I don't like this, Daisy,' he said. 'I want you to get back into the woods.'

'What for?'

'Just… just a feeling,' he muttered.

Suddenly a child's scream rang out.

Oliver and Daisy turned to see a woman grabbing the child and dragging it back towards her as the air around them… shimmered. Like a haze, a mirage on a hot day.

Out of that haze stepped… *something*.

And in less than a second, there were about twenty... somethings surrounding the green, blocking off Daisy's potential escape route back to the woods.

More people began emerging from their homes in the village and, as they did so, more hazes appeared, and more... things.

It didn't take Oliver long to realise that the village was now cut off entirely. Every road or pathway was blocked, guarded by strange people in dark red uniforms that seemed to be sculpted to their bodies. They were physically strong by the look of it: each of them stood about six foot six, heads hidden beneath black reflective helmets of a type he'd never seen.

They had no insignia on their uniforms, but each wore a wide black belt with many pouches, and a couple had bandoliers from belt to right shoulder. Every single one of them carried what looked like a rifle, only far shorter and thicker. They carried them in one hand and were using them to herd the villagers towards the green.

One man suddenly stopped – Oliver recognised him from the pub. He wasn't the landlord but he helped behind the bar. Oliver had liked him; he was like one of the men from the trenches. From the War.

Oh God. Was this some new German atrocity in the making, ten years on? He had heard the rumours of course, but dismissed them. Why would anyone want to start another conflict after the Great War had left Europe so utterly bereft?

The man from the pub suddenly swung a punch at the uniformed guard pushing him forward.

The red guard brought up his gun and fired.

Oliver expected to hear a gunshot, that awful explosion of powder and spark propelling hot death that, at that range, would have drilled through the pub man's heart in a second. But there was no gunshot. Instead there was a roar, like a gas flame suddenly ignited at a hundred times normal volume.

In the time it took the pub man's body to jerk back from the shot's impact, his clothing and skin had just gone. A charred skeleton took an involuntary final step backwards before starting to topple to the ground.

Worse still, the skeleton never made it. It seemed just to fade to ash and dissipate on the breeze. Where once a human being had stood, now there was no evidence he had ever existed.

Then hell broke loose.

People ran, screaming. Men, women, children, tried to flee in all directions. To their homes. Away from the green. From the village. One by one they vanished, utterly vaporised by these hideous guns.

Houses, cars, shops, all exploded as the enemy guns spat whatever death it was they spat. Huge geysers of fire erupted over the ground, the green, the roads as the guns kept firing.

As Oliver tried to comprehend what was

happening, he felt Daisy tug on his arm. 'Run!' she screamed in his ear. 'The woods!'

But Oliver had realised that running was pointless; it only aggravated these villains. 'No,' he hissed. 'Stay still.'

He never took his eyes off the red uniformed... things as they walked towards him.

He felt Daisy hit his wrist, trying to provoke him to move. But he couldn't, he was rooted to the spot as the whole village became a burning pyre, a massive enclosure of death and destruction around him. He was dimly aware that even the woods were aflame now.

'There's no way through,' he managed to mutter to Daisy. When she didn't respond, he finally turned to look at her.

She was gone.

Not in a running-away sense. He felt it in his chest, in his heart.

She was, like all the others, dead. Gone for ever.

He knew this because, although in his head he could still remember her grabbing his arm, he realised that the thump on his wrist hadn't been her trying to get him to move. It had been the moment Daisy Conlan had been vaporised like everyone else.

And she had taken his left hand and wrist along with her.

In shock, in utter disbelief, he raised his left arm, staring at the cauterised stump. He wanted to laugh.

Even his wristwatch was gone. A gift from his late mother, six years ago on his 27th birthday.

He wanted to scream, to cry out in anguish at her death. Instead, all that went through his mind was 'What do I tell her father?'

Then everything stopped. The explosions, the screams of violent death, the flashes of fire, that noise… that terrible, terrible noise, that terrible, terrible roar of the guns that echoed around in his head, that wouldn't stop, wouldn't cease. He could hear it, smell the burning flesh, see the devastated village that was already nothing more than ripped up roads, grass and shattered buildings.

The village had been utterly devastated in less than a minute.

Oliver was on his knees, sobbing and screaming in equal measure, his own voice in his head echoing around with the roar of the guns and the long-extinguished screams of the dying that he and he alone could still hear.

He wasn't really aware of the red guard in front of him, that reached up and touched its helmet. The helmet shimmered and vanished, and in its place was a twisted inhuman face that seemed to be pickled, like a prune, or flesh that had been left in bathwater for many days.

Two red eyes bore into Oliver's face. A thin slit of a mouth twisted open, and Oliver felt the breath on his face. Harsh breath, like gas and ignited petroleum in one.

'Where are they?' it demanded of Oliver. 'We know you are sheltering them somewhere on this planet. Where are the Weave?'

Oliver couldn't answer. He didn't understand the question.

'They are in this quadrant, on this island,' he heard the creature bellow suddenly, clear and distinct.

And then Oliver's life was changed for ever.

All he could hear were roaring guns, screaming people and skeletons burning.

All he could smell was the creature's breath.

All he could think about was Daisy dying by his side.

He began to scream. Whether it was just in his head or out loud, he couldn't tell.

His mind switched off, and the last thing he remembered was silence. Utter silence. As if the sounds of the universe had been switched off.

Complete silence. Other than his own hoarse screaming, of course.

His one palm had pressed into the scorched earth of the green and he felt the heavy tread of the creatures as they moved away.

And Oliver let everything go and allowed the darkness to take him.

Chapter
3

It was so dark, so cold in the ship. How long had they been here, wherever here was? Surely the chamber should have opened by now? She'd been awake for over thirty minutes – it was designed to open after fifteen, by which time their bodies should be acclimatised.

Something was wrong.

She sniffed: stale air inside the chamber and… damp. Damp was the worst thing that could happen. The chambers were supposed to be protected against this.

She realised she could move her hands and raised them, immediately discovering that she was pressed against the lid of the chamber – either she'd put on a lot of weight while asleep or the chamber had shrunk. Both of these were unlikely, so there had to be another explanation.

Slowly she started feeling around in the dark until she found the control switches, but they were dead. They had enough power to outlive aeons. Something was definitely wrong.

She took a deep breath and smashed upwards with her hands, and the chamber's lid flew straight upwards, which gave her her first shock. Her second shock came when she started to follow the lid, realising as her body started to lunge forward that the chamber hadn't shrunk at all: it was suspended upside down or at an angle of some sort. About seventy degrees was the estimate that shot though her mind as she fell the short distance to the floor.

The lid clattered noisily onto the far wall that now acted as the floor. The ambient yellow light suggested that, although the controls had failed, there must still be emergency lighting. She looked for its source and saw a jury-rigged lamp had been suspended from another open casket at the same angle. 3's. Good for him – up and about already, and using his brain.

All the ship's controls must have failed if a battery light was their only source of illumination. The lamp was dim, so it could've been in use for hours. Days possibly, though not much more than a week.

She called 3's name but got no reply.

She felt hungry. Thirsty too. That was weird – the suspension should have kept her full of vitamins, but she was tired, aching. Suspension sickness – not everyone got it, but clearly fate wasn't going to be kind to her today. Oh well, easily cured with the right medicine. Hmm... She couldn't work out which chambers contained the medical staff.

This wasn't looking good. Nor, frankly, was the fact the ship was upturned. That was why she couldn't see into the chambers from so far down – and 3's was apparently the only other open chamber.

128 sighed. If they were to have a chance of re-growing the ship to working order and getting away from wherever they had crashed, she needed everyone in tip-top condition. Not least herself.

She reached out to the wall-floor beneath her and created a small hole in it by absorption.

Darkness. A solid darkness. She risked putting her hand through and discovered that whatever was beyond the wall was cold and damp but not lethal. Maybe that was where the damp had come from that she'd felt inside her cryogenic chamber. Either way, cold and damp was not going to be a friend to her crew.

She tried to think – who had been next to her? 25463? Yes. Good. He'd been on her left, and to her right had been a young engineer. 282389, she thought.

She took a leap, trying to get back to her open chamber, allowing herself to extend slightly, just enough to reach it without using up valuable energy. Normally, she wouldn't have thought twice about expanding but, in her current state, she'd lose cohesion if she expended too much energy.

She pulled herself up so she was hanging outwards from her chamber, feet inside it, and used her left arm to reach over to 25463's chamber, thumping the emergency manual-release coil. Sure enough, the chamber lid flipped up and she reached forward to stop her Tactical Officer dropping forward as she had.

She felt him breathe under her hand and waited patiently as he started to come round.

'We made it, then,' he said.

'Yeah, good to see you, too,' 128 smiled. 'Taciturn as ever. Good to know nothing changes.'

She filled him in – as much as she knew – while he slowly clambered down to the floor.

'We need to find one of the medical staff,' he said. '107863 or 49 would be good. Or a nurse even. 9726 was prettiest.' He glanced around. 'Then I want my security team here. Once we have those essentials, we can try bringing the rest of the crew round with medics to help them and my security team ready to find out where we are.'

Before the Commander could answer, a voice made them turn.

'We're on a planet called Earth. Strictly speaking, we're under it.'

128 wanted to hug 3, but instead she just asked for a report.

3 had awoken two days earlier. Much like 128, he'd felt the cold and damp but had chosen to gather information rather than wake the crew as his rank's protocol required. 'I couldn't remember which chamber 8's team were in, so it was a gamble,' he added wryly.

'It was,' 25463 snapped. 'My Security Chief should have been your priority. If anything had happened to you—'

'Yeah, but it didn't. The *Exalted* is damaged but not irreparably, provided we have a full complement of crew.'

'Do we have spares?'

'Most of the Balls were damaged, but there's a limited number. A lot of our spares were used to protect us on descent, I reckon.'

'Any sign of Tahnn activity? Were we followed?'

3 shrugged. 'If we were, Commander, they're certainly not around here, or we'd be dead.'

'What's the indigenous population at?'

'Level 5, I reckon. I smell engine oil but nothing neutronic or atomic in the air. The primary life form is reasonably civilised, in that they don't appear to be eating one another, but I doubt they've seen non-local life before, so I'm not proposing we run out and shake hands with them.'

'We won't learn anything by skulking down here,' retorted 25463.

'Children,' snapped the Commander. 'Don't start. 25463, start getting the crew up. Who and when, I leave to you. 3, take me out there – I want to see an alien world.'

'Commander, I'm not sure—'

'Don't argue, Exec. I'm still the Commander.' She winked at him. 'This is fun.'

'This is dangerous.'

'That too.' 128 threw a look back at 25463, who was starting to track down his security team and a couple of nurses as planned. 'Let's go,' she told her second-in-command, 'before he gets any more miserable.'

'You could almost believe he wanted to fail and die,' 3 muttered.

'Don't say that,' 128 said taking his arm sharply. 'Don't ever say that about him or any of the *Exalted* crew. Because it's not true. We will survive this, and we will find a way home, no matter how long it takes.'

3 indicated that he accepted the criticism and extracted his arm. 'This way, Commander,' he said.

128 sighed to herself. Why did everyone have to make everything so difficult? It suddenly occurred to her exactly what it was she was about to do. It was both exciting and dangerous. She reached into her uniform and found the small homing beacon.

'Let's get some help,' she said to 3. 'Just in case.' She activated the beacon.

After a few moments, they reached a hole that 3 had dug. The smell hit her before the bright daylight, but together they were almost overwhelming.

'It's a whole new planet, 3,' she breathed. 'Look at it.'

The sky was blue and white and slightly yellow, the ground green and brown and black and… and there were buildings of non-conformed shapes and sizes in the distance.

'Flowers,' she said, reaching for a white and yellow plant, but 3 held her back.

'Commander, I've had no way to test anything. Other than not actually suffocating and feeling the damp in the air – which means we can't stay long in our natural state, by the way – I've touched nothing. We don't know what it can do.'

'We are explorers, 3. This is what we do.' She reached out and plucked the plant from the ground, hoping this wasn't the primary life form to which 3 had referred, otherwise her first action on this planet was murder. Then she remembered that 3 had said it was planet Earth, so the natives had to have communication.

As if reading her mind, 3 pointed to the buildings. 'Creatures, not too unlike ourselves, in shape and size, live over there. A couple of dozen, I reckon. There's no conformity to their clothing or anything.'

128 wanted to shriek with excitement, but even in front of 3 that wouldn't be de rigueur for a Commander. Especially a Commander that had just chastised her Exec Officer for being too flippant. She looked at the plant in her hand and let it melt into

her palm, closing her eyes and focusing.

'Simple cell structure, mostly carbon, oxygen and water.' She opened her eyes and smiled again. 'Easy to replicate. Which means that – assuming it's like our planet – carbon, oxygen and water are the main ingredients of everything living here. We can infiltrate easily once we have a template of the natives.' She looked at 3. 'Fancy a mission?'

'How many of them do you want, Commander?'

'Just one for now. We don't want to scare them or hurt them. But we have to know if we can replicate them.'

'Why?'

'Because if we end up being here a few days, weeks or years, we will need to be out and about and, to do that, we need to look, speak and think like them.' 128 smiled. 'I'll see you back here in thirty minutes.'

With a nod, 3 walked out into the bright day of this strange new planet. 128 watched his departing back with pride. He wouldn't let her down. He wouldn't let the crew down. He wouldn't let the Weave down.

She suddenly gasped in pain – damn suspension sickness was coming up fast. She needed to flow urgently, but to do that she'd need a nurse.

She was aware of someone at her side and relaxed. Nurse 66663.

'Commander,' said the young male nurse, '25463 wondered if you needed sickness suppressants?'

The Commander nodded. 'You are a life saver 66663, thank you.'

The nurse pressed a small soft patch against the Commander's arm, and she immediately felt the soothing sensation through her fibres. 'Thank you, 66663. Tend to the others.'

As the nurse was about to head back beneath the ground, 128 caught his arm. 'Is everyone OK?' she asked.

The nurse paused just for a beat. 'Yes, Commander.'

128 sighed. 'The truth, nurse, please.' But she knew 25463 would have ordered him not to reveal it. 'It's all right, nurse, I'll ask him myself.'

She followed the nurse back, throwing one quick look behind her to the open air, but 3's form had already vanished amidst the new world's myriad secrets and promises.

Within moments, they had returned to the upturned ship and the suspended chambers. Only three were untouched, and one of those was being prised open by some of the security team.

The Commander was relieved to see 79 was there – she liked the young geographer. And the artists 1419 and 2296 were around, too, holding hands just as lovingly as they had on the day the Commander had performed their wedding ceremony.

25463 was anxiously pacing, and he pulled 128 to one side, more roughly than he probably intended. She didn't reprimand him.

'I'm concerned about those three,' he said nodding at the unopened chambers. 'It's been too long, and all the others opened with ease. Chief 8 believes that the chambers may have been damaged in the crash.'

128 did a quick scan. '174526, 207 and 542,' she said, blowing air from her cheeks.

There was a cry from 8, the Security Chief, and the lid of the casket was finally prised free. With a screech of fear and panic, the male occupant sat bolt upright and was stopped by Chief 8 from falling out. 'You're OK, you're OK,' he kept repeating to the older man calmly.

128 sighed in relief. The astrometrist, 207. One down, two to go.

A couple of 8's burly lads were desperately trying to get the next lid off, but it wouldn't budge. One of them, 19, produced a sidearm in his hand, gasping slightly from the strain. He was tired – probably only revived himself scant moments before, too soon to be growing armaments. But he wasn't thinking of his own health when someone else was in danger. He carefully heated up the runners of the sliding mechanism, and eventually it came loose enough for his partner, 11, to haul the chamber's lid away.

There was no happy yell or coughing this time, and 128 could tell the occupant was dead before either man reacted.

'Grieve later,' snapped 8 urgently. 'Let's get the final one sorted.'

One more blast from the gun – and another pyrrhic victory – later and the Commander found herself and her crew (minus EO 3) looking at two corpses at their feet. Both were frayed and unwoven beyond recognition, but their uniform badges IDed them: on the left was Chief Engineer 174526; on the right was junior science officer 542.

The Commander said a few words about 174526 and death in general, then allowed Nurse 9726 to speak about 542, her brother.

When it was over, the Commander kneeled down, placed both palms to the ship's floor-wall and concentrated. A second later, the remains of the two bodies were absorbed by the ship.

'We can't stay here,' 128 said. 'I propose taking a small party to the world outside and, once 3 has returned with a template, I suggest we integrate ourselves with the planet until we can find a way to repair and repower the ship. Myself, 8, 19, 30, 877, 107863 and 41200 will come with me. Tactical Officer 25463 is in charge with Security Chief 8 as deputy until either myself or Exec Officer 3 return.'

25463 was about to argue, but 128 threw him a look. 'I need you here, looking after my crew. If anything goes wrong, you are to stay awake as long as possible to reenergise yourselves then return to hibernation. But, of course, nothing will go wrong.' She smiled at the crew. Her crew. The best. And they looked back, their faces a mixture of pride, determination, fear, anxiety, serenity and, in one case, downright pig-headedness. 'You are the best,' she said to them, then turned to her sub-group. 'Let's go, team.'

As she started to follow them out, she took 25463's hand. 'Look after them. We'll be back in three days, tops.'

She walked away, without looking back, hoping that 3 would not be long and that he would soon join them on their venture into the unknown.

CHAPTER
4

Baaaaa

'What?'

Baaaaaaa

'I see. Rory?'

Baaaaa

'Nope. No, definitely not Rory. Although I can see some similarities. F'rinstance, you're standing there, gazing at me, assuming I know what's going on. And making strange noises that no one understands. But I'm pretty sure, despite all that, you're not Rory.'

'Ummmm, Doctor?'

'Ahhh, see, now *that's* Rory. But you see what I was getting at, yes?'

Baaaaaa

'Doctor?'

'Quiet, Rory. I'm talking to a sheep.'

Baaaaa

'All right, strictly speaking, I'm talking *at* a sheep, but I'm pretty sure I'm getting through.' The Doctor sniffed. 'Blimey, Mr Sheep, you smell bad. No... wait... nope, you're all right, *I* smell bad. Wow. That *is* bad. Sorry.'

Baaaa

'Absolutely.'

Rory's next call was tinged with desperation. 'Doctor...'

'What?'

'You've, ummm... well, you're in... ummm...'

'I'm in sheep dip, Rory, aren't I?'

'Yup.'

'Why am I in sheep dip, Rory? No, wait, it doesn't matter, I don't care. Because I reckon that whatever answer you give, I'm not gonna like it much. And neither of us will come out of any subsequent discussions on the subject particularly well, am I right?'

'No, Doctor.'

'Where's Amy? How come she's not in sheep dip? She always knows how to deal with me in situations like this. Me. Sheep dip. Bad smells.'

Baaaa

'And you, frankly, Mr Sheep, aren't helping matters much.'

'Doctor!'

'*What?*'

Rory sighed. Loudly. He did that a lot. 'Apart from the dip, and the sheep, and the rather steep hill you just fell down – and trust me you don't want to go into whatever it was you trod on that caused you to fall down—'

'Get on with it, Rory, I'm not getting drier or happier down here.'

'Well, anyway, there's a man up here, and I don't think he's too chuffed.'

'Is he a shepherd, by any chance? I mean, right now, a man whose passport lists "shepherd" as an occupation might be really useful.'

'He's got a shotgun. Aimed at me.'

'Try not to get shot, then, Rory. Can you manage that? Amy won't thank me if you get shot.'

'I won't thank you, either,' Rory countered.

'You'll be dead.'

'There is that,' Rory answered. 'And thanks for the vote of confidence. You're a bundle of fun today.'

Baaaa

The Doctor sighed. 'And you, my woolly friend, aren't exactly helping.'

With a big squelching noise, the Doctor hauled himself out of the dip and promptly fell flat on his back. He looked up at the blue, cloudless sky above and sniffed. 'Overlooking the sheep-dip smell – which isn't so bad once you get used to it – I can smell a good cut-grass smell. Earth, England.' Another sniff. 'Gotta be the east coast, low down. We're in Norfolk, Rory. Suffolk at a push.' He smiled at the sheep. 'Don't get sheep on many other planets. You are pretty much unique.'

He pushed himself up onto his elbows. 'It's quite nice down here, actually,' he called back up the hillock to where he thought Rory must be. 'You should take the time to look at the sky more often. Smell the grass, taste English air on the tip of your tongue. Marvellous.'

'You're forgetting something, Doctor,' yelled Rory. 'Shotgun. Me. Danger?'

'If he was going to shoot you, Rory, he'd've done it by now. So it's an empty threat. A threat, yes, but pretty empty. English farmers are the ask-questions-first-shoot-later types.' The Doctor looked at his neighbour, the sheep. 'I think that's the right way around, anyway,' he said with a confidential wink.

Baaaa

'Yes, OK, you're right, I'd better get up there and get Rory out of whatever mess he's in this week.'

The Doctor was on his feet, straightening his bow tie and brushing those bits of sheep dip from his clothes that could be easily brushed off, pausing only to wipe his now mucky hands on the grass. With a last look at the sheep and a nod of goodbye, he began climbing back up the hillock he'd taken his tumble down.

The TARDIS had arrived just a few moments earlier, he remembered. He'd checked the atmosphere and walked out. 'Pretty sure I looked where I was going,' he muttered in a voice that implied he wasn't sure of that at all.

As the TARDIS came into view, door wide open, he realised his mistake – he had indeed walked straight out and down, because the door was on the edge of the top of the hill. 'Quite a tumble,' he said. Then: 'I said I took quite a tumble,' he yelled towards where he had now worked out Rory definitely was. He and Amy had presumably been a bit more circumspect in leaving the ship. Wise, if dull.

With a last grunt of effort, the Doctor reached the apex of the hill, by his faithful TARDIS.

Rory was sat cross-legged on the grass a way off, hands on his head. Two men were standing there: a really rather young farmer (flat cap – such a cliché, but it dated him, somewhere mid twentieth century, most likely) and a gentleman (tweeds, breeches, equally clichéd but cut very well – this was between the wars, definitely).

'Hullo,' he called cheerily. 'See you've met my mate Rory. Sorry, are we trespassing, I didn't see the signs and Rory, well, I'm not sure if he can read.' He tapped the side of his head. 'Not really all there, dropped on his head as a baby, I reckon.'

'Oi,' moaned Rory. 'I can hear you, you know.'

The Doctor shook his head. 'I was attempting to be charming, disarming even. Putting these fine people at their ease. And giving them a good reason not to blow your brains out.'

'Oh. Sorry.'

The Doctor walked over to the gentleman –

landowner, maybe – casually brushing past the shotgun as he did so and somehow easing it from the young farmer's hand, breaking it, tipping the shotgun shells out onto his palm before pocketing them, closing it and handing it back – so it was once again aimed at Rory, albeit impotently. All in one fluid movement, topped off with a friendly nod.

'Stay put,' he told Rory. 'Just to be polite.'

The farmer lowered the useless shotgun, but Rory stayed put.

The Doctor offered his hand to the gentleman. 'Lovely field you've got here. I'm the Doctor. That, as you may have gathered, is Rory Williams. Somewhere around here should be another chum, Amy Pond. Tall, redhead, Scots – but we try not to hold that against her too much. Very nice. She and Rory are getting married in about seventy-five years, give or take.'

The gentleman didn't proffer his hand in return but just nodded. 'I see. Name's Porter, Nathaniel Porter. I own this land.'

'Yes!' exclaimed the Doctor, pleased he'd guessed correctly. '*Smokin'*.'

No one reacted other than Rory, who sighed, rather melodramatically.

'OK, another word crossed off the list, Rory,' the Doctor acknowledged. He looked at Nathaniel Porter and winked, then gestured expansively. 'Nice land to own, I must say, and I'm terribly sorry we trespassed. Allow me to assure you it was quite unintentional.' He leaned in to the landowner. 'I blame Rory. He always leads us up the wrong path.'

'What's that doing here? Setting up a campsite, were you?'

This came from the young farmer with the flat cap and useless shotgun. He was pointing at the TARDIS.

The Doctor produced the wallet that contained his psychic paper and showed it to Nathaniel Porter, who stared at it and nodded. 'Benson,' he said, 'Take a look at this, young man, and see if you agree with the credentials.'

The young farmer crossed to them, read the paper and raised an eyebrow. 'Scotland Yard? Is it about the dig? The complaints?'

The Doctor nodded. 'We were trying to set up a small outpost, but I think we ended up in the wrong field. Wanted it to be hush-hush.' The Doctor reached out and helped Rory up. 'Rory's on loan from Gloucester University's geological department.'

'Sorry about the sheep dip,' Rory said to Benson. 'The Doctor must have slipped as we set our police box up.'

The Doctor smiled at Rory. 'I get clumsy when I'm in the countryside. Bit of a city boy, really.' He looked back at Nathaniel Porter and stared at him, just for a split second too long. Then spoke. 'So, anyway, we need to find WPC Pond.'

Benson frowned. 'WPC?'

'Yeah,' Rory said. 'Always wanted to join the force, ever since she was a little girl. Looks great in the uniform.'

The Doctor threw Rory a look. 'The Stanley look isn't her favourite, actually, so she's in civilian clothing whilst we're here. Trying to blend in.' He sighed at the jeans and *Space Invaders* T-shirt Rory was wearing. 'An art not everyone has mastered, it seems.'

'What's she wearing?' Nathaniel Porter asked. 'Benson can get his fellow farmhands to keep an eye out. Won't have wandered far, but the villagers are a bit… unsure of strangers.'

The Doctor nodded. 'Absolutely. Rory?'

'Umm…' Rory tried to remember. 'Blue baggy top, short black skirt. Trainers.'

'Oh that's so very 1930s,' the Doctor muttered, adding to Benson, 'All the rage in London. Probably won't take off here for, oh, lots of years.' He sniffed. 'What's that smell?'

'It's you,' answered Rory. 'Sheep dip.'

'You need a bath, Doctor,' said Nathaniel Porter. 'Follow me back to the Manse, soon get you sorted.'

The Doctor and Rory nodded and started to follow.

'I'll find your Miss Pond,' Benson called. 'And when I do, I'll point her in your direction.'

The Doctor turned and shook his hand. 'Thank you.'

Benson shook it back and wandered off.

Keeping a distance between Nathaniel Porter and themselves, the Doctor and Rory were able to talk quietly.

'So, one shakes hands and one doesn't,' said the Doctor. 'That's two odd things about our host.'

'And the other?'

'Oh, think about what you saw, Rory. Think and realise.'

Rory frowned as he mentally skipped through the past few minutes, but shrugged.

With a smile, the Doctor waved his wallet with the psychic paper in it. 'He's the landowner, probably runs the entire village, lives in a Manse, may be the Vicar as well. Bet he's a magistrate, they always were in these days. So why'd he show our documentation to the hired help?'

'The farmer? I don't know. Maybe Porter can't read.'

The Doctor sighed. 'I doubt that's the problem.'

Then Rory nodded. 'Because the psychic paper didn't work on him. He needed the farmer to see what it said. To him, it was just blank.'

'You're learning, Rory. I'm proud of you.'

Rory started to smile, then frowned. 'Don't patronise me, Doctor.'

But the Doctor was lost in thought. 'So, either he has the most closed mind on Earth, or he's a genius, or he has no imagination, or... *or* he's trained not to be psychic-papered. Which is pretty rare in 1930s

Norfolk, I reckon.'

'1930s?'

The Doctor dug his hand into his pockets and brought out the shotgun cartridges. 'Didn't make them like this till the late twenties; by the time war broke out, they'd changed again.' He put his finger into the cartridge then out again, licking tiny fragments of shot off it. 'Yup,' he said, licking his lips rapidly, like a lizard, to get rid of the taste. 'Vile stuff. 1930s. Deffo. 1936, I reckon.'

Rory pointed ahead. 'Nice village, though. Like home.'

The Doctor nodded. 'One more thing. Our host lives in a Manse. What's missing from that view?'

Rory gazed at the village in the bowl-like area beneath them as they started down a small hill towards it. 'Shopping mall?' he said lamely.

'No church. How many typical English villages have you been to that don't have churches but have a Manse?' The Doctor stared at Rory. 'You know what a Manse is? Posh vicarage. All the rage in villages in England in the 1930s. Well, those with churches. No need for a vicarage if there's no vicar, I'd've thought. You agree?'

If Rory was about to point out he'd never actually been to a village in the 1930s at all, let alone thought about the significance of manses, churches or otherwise, he never got the chance because the Doctor was grabbing his arm excitedly and pointing at a couple of conjoined red-brick buildings on the far left of the place. To one side of that, within its grounds, a huge pile of earth had been built up.

'It looks like *Time Team*,' Rory said.

The Doctor nodded. 'An archaeological dig in the playing field of what I'm guessing is the local school. How exciting is that?'

'Oh. Very, Doctor,' Rory lied. 'You said we'd come here cos of a distress beacon the TARDIS located,' he added under his breath.

Suddenly Nathaniel Porter stopped, perhaps because he'd seen what the Doctor had seen. Hopefully not because he'd heard Rory mention distress beacons.

'One imagines that is why you are here, Doctor. To sort out the problems created by the dig?'

'Unpopular, Mr Porter?'

Porter nodded. 'You could say that. Enola has had no end of trouble from some of the locals and a number of out-of-towners. That's why we sent for the police in the first place.'

'Enola?'

'My wife,' he said proudly. 'My second, and most beautiful, wife. And the most thrilling archaeologist of the day.'

'I can't wait to meet her,' the Doctor said.

'The Manse is this way,' Nathaniel Porter said, pointing towards the opposite end of the village from the school. 'Have a good scrub down, and you'll meet her when you join us for dinner tonight. I say, you got lodgings sorted?'

'Not yet,' said Rory.

'Marvellous. The three of you can stay with us then. Plenty of rooms at the Manse,' Porter called after them.

'Oh, thank you, Mr Porter,' said Amy Pond, linking an arm through Rory's. 'That saves everyone a lot of problems.'

'Hullo, Amy.' The Doctor smiled. 'Where did you get to?'

'You missed the Doctor trying to talk to a sheep,' Rory laughed.

'Really? Wow, now I bet the sheep gave as good as he got.'

Rory shrugged. 'I think they were on the same level, certainly. Intellectually as well as physically.'

'Oi. You don't know me well enough to insult me, Rory Williams.'

'You insult me all the time,' Rory protested.

'That's true, you do,' Amy nodded. 'And he's my hubbie-to-be, so I have to defer to him on this one or he may leave me at the altar.'

The Doctor laughed. 'If you ever get to the altar. I may just abandon you here in 1936. Yeah, bet you didn't consider that when you were thinking up new ways to insult the poor old Doctor.'

Rory was going to respond but Amy winked at him then rested her head on the Doctor's shoulder. 'Awww, is poor ickle Doctor getting picked on by the nasty humans?'

'Yes he is. I wonder why I always think this is

my favourite planet. It's full of horrible people.' He grinned. 'But I suppose there are one or two who are better than the rest.'

'Could be worse,' Amy said. 'Imagine if Mars was your favourite planet. No one there to travel with you.'

The Doctor's smile faltered just for a second.

'Doctor?' Rory said concerned.

'Nothing,' he said. 'Mars. Not my favourite, to be honest.' He looked at Amy. 'And you'd be surprised what you can find on Mars, go back far enough.' Then he grinned a marvellously huge grin and threw his arms around the shoulders of his friends. 'And now my best friends are covered in sheep dip too!'

They laughed together and kept walking, taking in the English countryside as they headed towards the village. Then the Doctor stopped. His companions stopped too, because they could sense the Doctor's sudden... trepidation?

'What's up?'

The Doctor held up a hand to shush them, cocking his head slightly.

'I can't hear anything...' Rory started, but the Doctor waved him quiet.

'No, Rory, you're right,' he finally said. 'We're in an English village. On a Sunday morning. With a dig. And three strangers arrive in a field in a big blue box. And no one's making a sound. Quietest village in the world, I reckon.'

'P'raps they're all watching telly in the pub?' offered Rory.

'1936,' countered the Doctor.

'Listening to the radio?'

'1936,' said Amy. 'Not much on.'

'BBC's quite new,' the Doctor explained. 'And out here, the radio market's not quite so big.'

'So why is it so quiet?'

The Doctor smiled at his friends. 'Let's find out.'

'Or... I have a better plan,' said Rory.

'What's that then?' asked Amy.

'Let's ask Nathaniel Porter.'

The Doctor turned to see their host a little way behind them, just standing there. Watching them.

'Now, what would be the fun in that?' he said. 'I bet he has all the answers.'

'Umm, we want answers?' Amy said.

'Ah yes. Well, yes, we do. But, ask yourself this, do we want his answers or our answers?'

'You're sure they'd be so different?'

'Of course I am. He's the headman, the big boss, the lord and master of whatever this quaint little place is called. He'll have the best answers going. But I bet they're a bit boring.'

Nathaniel Porter caught them up, a big grin on his face. 'The Manse is this way,' he said, pointing away from the school, and down a long road.

He crossed in front of them and into the village, and the others followed.

As soon as they were on solid road rather than

grass and mud, Rory felt... different. He couldn't explain it, so he chose not to say anything to Amy or the Doctor. But he felt something. Like someone had just walked over his grave.

He hoped this wasn't a portent.

Chapter
5

They were greeted at the Manse, Nathaniel Porter's vast house, by a man who took great pains to point out, when the Doctor mentioned it, that he wasn't a butler but a gentleman's manservant.

Rory wasn't quite sure what the difference was, but decided that whatever kept the man happy was fine with him. He couldn't be sure if his name was Chidders or Chinners because he spoke with a broad Norfolk accent. (Well, Rory assumed it was a broad Norfolk accent – he wasn't entirely sure he'd know a Norfolk accent if he tripped over it – but it was an accent and very broad.)

Nathaniel Porter himself was a strange man. He was tall and powerfully built, and he carried himself much as Rory expected a Lord of the Manor to carry himself. Porter was explaining that the Manse had been personally designed by its original owner in 1824 to suit 'his eccentric attitudes'. As local legend had it, Porter told them, calling it 'the Manse' had been a sort of 1824 joke at the expense of a village with no consecrated ground and thus no church or graveyard. 'One of the mysteries of Shalford Heights,' he said pompously, which at least told them where exactly they were.

The Manse wasn't exactly a manor – it was mostly a one-level house, with the only two-storey element being at one side, up a grand staircase leading to what Nathaniel Porter told them were his 'personal rooms'. The front door took them into a semicircular hallway, to the right of which was a small door leading to the kitchen. Beyond that, ranged at equal points, were three corridors that seemed to go straight into darkness. Porter said each corridor led to what he termed a wing – the first led to his study and 'private rooms', and something in the tone of his voice told Rory it was off-limits. Rory knew that, if the Doctor thought the same, it was going to be the first place he'd be trying to explore.

The second corridor led to a small set of guest rooms. At the apex of this were two framed photographs.

'One is Mrs Porter, I imagine?' the Doctor mused.

Nathaniel Porter nodded. 'And my first wife. The staff like to keep them there, watching over them almost, and Enola doesn't mind. She's not threatened by my past.'

Rory thought that was an odd thing to say, especially to three virtual strangers. Perhaps Nathaniel Porter wasn't used to having house guests. Or perhaps he was just a bit weird.

'Wow, there's quite an age difference,' Amy said. 'You old dog,' she winked at their host, tapping the one of Enola.

Nathaniel Porter just looked at the Doctor and said that the third passageway led to a dining room and drawing room that looked out onto the 'magnificent walled garden'.

'And the fourth,' Porter concluded proudly, 'leads to a set of private rooms for my permanent guest.'

He sounded as if he was describing a beloved pet or a child. Whatever, Rory decided, it was a weird way to talk about a guest.

'His name is Oliver Marks. He was a… a friend of my first wife.'

'Ooh,' said Amy. 'So where is the first Mrs Porter? Under the patio?'

The Doctor shot her a look. '1936,' he hissed. Then he was all smiles to Nathaniel Porter. 'Ignore Miss Pond, Mr Porter,' he said. 'I'm sorry, we didn't mean to be rude about the first Mrs Porter.'

'These things happen, Doctor,' Nathaniel Porter replied. Then he glanced at Amy. 'And no, Miss Pond, not under the patio. But with no churchyard, she is not buried locally.'

Amy gave Rory an *oooh, I've done it now* look, and he tried to smile comfortingly at her, but she was already back to staring round the hallway, spotting some paintings on the walls. 'So, who're this lot, then? Family portraits?' she said, moving on quickly from her faux pas.

Their host shrugged. 'To be honest, I have no idea. They were in the Manse when I obtained it and I have never enquired. I just kept them up as decoration.' He bowed slightly. 'If you will excuse me, I must freshen up before lunch. My man will show you your rooms, then Mrs Stern will provide us with platters of cold meats and salads, if that is satisfactory?'

'More than,' the Doctor said. 'Thank you.'

And Cheggers, or whoever he was, led them down a long, dark and thin corridor that seemed straight but, when Rory looked over his shoulder back to the hallway, he only saw darkness, meaning they must have veered slightly to the left or right without realising it.

Weird place.

Cheggers stopped in the corridor, facing the three friends and pointing at opposite doors. 'Your rooms,' he said.

Rory was about to point out that he and Amy could share when she smiled at him. '1936,' she said, mimicking the Doctor earlier.

Amy took the left-hand room. With a sigh of resignation, Rory went right. He didn't see where the Doctor went but quickly realised he was next door – seconds after he'd closed the door to the corridor, a connecting door in his room burst open to reveal the Doctor standing there.

'No en suite,' the Doctor said. 'Shame. Only three stars for this hotel, then.'

'What's going on?' Rory demanded. 'I mean, why are we here?'

'No idea, Rory.'

'But you brought us here.'

'The TARDIS did.'

'Don't be smart,' Rory snapped. 'You pilot the TARDIS. You brought us here.'

'Actually, this time I didn't. I promised you Rio, and we got Norfolk.'

'I didn't believe you really meant to take us to Rio.'

'But I said I would!'

'Yeah. Last time you said Rio, we ended up in Tibet. The time before, it's a world of dragons and jousting. I'm not sure if Rio is in Brazil or is actually some mysterious distant galaxy that's just called Rio to confuse us.'

There was a gentle tap on the door, and both men said 'Come in, Amy' simultaneously.

'Sorry,' the Doctor said to Rory. 'Your room, your calling out "come in" thingy, right, permission stuff.'

'My girlfriend, too,' Rory added although he wasn't quite sure why.

'Aww, are my boys fighting over me?' Amy said as she came in. 'And I think he means Rio in Brazil.'

Rory and the Doctor frowned at her.

'Old house, but thin walls and doors. Who knew?' Amy sat on Rory's bed so he sat beside her. The Doctor stayed in the connecting doorway to his own room.

'Bite to eat, then exploring. Information-gathering time,' the Doctor said.

'You notice how *mein host* responded to my mention of the age difference between the old and new Mrs Porters?'

'Thankfully, he ignored you,' said Rory.

'Ah, but don't you see?' asked Amy. 'Anyone else would have reacted in some way. Said something. It was like... it was like it had never occurred to him.'

'Or,' offered the Doctor, 'he's too much of a gentleman to react to rude young Scots ladies. Particularly after making a joke about her being dead before knowing she actually was dead!'

Amy shrugged. 'I'm not convinced.'

'Anyway,' Rory tried to bring them back to the subject. 'Why are we here?'

The Doctor sighed. 'Not gonna let that one go, are you? I don't know, Rory. Which is weird for you, I'm sure, because you're used to me having all the answers, but I don't. Not this time.' He wrung his hands suddenly. 'And I don't like me not knowing any more than you like me not knowing. Not knowing is not good.'

'Hence post-lunch investigating,' Amy said. 'I can meet up with Tom, see what I can find out.'

'Good, you do that. Rory, I want you to go to the school. Bound to have a library, find out stuff.'

'Stuff? What sort of stuff?'

'Stuff stuff. Stuff about stuff. The sort of stuff that tells you stuff. Libraries are good at stuff.'

'OK,' Rory said. 'Stuff finding outing. After lunch.' He took Amy's hand, stroking the back of it gently, licked his lips and opened his mouth to speak then stopped.

'Rory?' Amy said.

'Well, I… you know…' He couldn't finish.

'If I may,' the Doctor said. 'I mean, your room, your rules, your girlfriend, but what I think Rory wants to know, Amy, is, ummm, who the hell is Tom?'

Rory nodded mutely. Because that was precisely what he wanted to know.

'Farmhand bloke,' she said. 'After you were finished messing around with sheep, he came and found me and pointed me in your direction. Said you'd spoken to him.'

'Oh,' the Doctor grinned. 'That Tom.' He looked more at Rory rather than Amy. 'Big, muscular, square-jawed Tom, nice tan from working in the fields all summer Tom. Big, strapping—'

'Yes, thank you, Doctor,' snapped Rory. 'I remember who Tom is.' He frowned at Amy. 'Why are you going on a date with Tom? Where's he taking you? When will you be back?'

'Ooh, not over-protective dad at all,' she said. 'He lives in the village, will know things. And is quite charming. And we have to get information. You get the library books, I get Farmer Tom. Handsome Farmer Tom.'

'Don't forget that tan,' the Doctor laughed.

Rory couldn't make up his mind whether he should be punching the Doctor, Tom or both of them, but what was the point?

His thoughts were interrupted when there was a tap on the door and the manservant entered. If he was surprised that all three were in Rory's room, he didn't let it show.

'Luncheon is served,' he said. 'The master will join you shortly but requests that you start without him.'

'Ooh, déjà vu!' Amy said suddenly. 'Seen that moment before!'

Rory raised an eyebrow. 'It's cliché day in Shalford Heights.'

The Doctor asked him what he meant, so he told them about his feeling of someone walking over his grave as they entered the village. 'But it probably happens all the time. It's only since hanging out with you, Doctor, that I've started looking for significance in the insignificant.'

'Ooh, very deep,' said the Doctor, slapping him on the back. 'So, lunch then, yes?' He looked to Nathaniel Porter's manservant for a beat and said,

'Lead on, sir.'

Instead, the man just pointed to his left and went right himself, away from the dining room.

The dining room, which was well lit with natural light from panoramic French doors which looked out onto a garden that, whilst not a disaster, had clearly seen better days. A magnificent willow tree was at the centre of the grassed area, tall and in full blossom, its skinny branches sweeping up and then down to the ground like a voluminous skirt that could hide anything within.

Rory remembered a school friend who'd had one like it. Alec. As kids, they'd run around his garden, hiding themselves among the tree's branches, pretending they were being eaten alive by a giant tree monster. Or it was the bridge of the Starship *Enterprise*. Or it was the caves that Indiana Jones would explore. Or it was the inside of the truck, as they waited to throw themselves out, armed to the teeth, catching the bank robbers in the act.

Years later, Rory had discovered Alec in a ward at work, victim of a car accident on the M5. He sat with Alec as much as possible, and they talked about their childhood, about friends they'd lost contact with as they'd grown up. Grown apart. When alien, human-eating tree monsters were no longer as important as CDs, DVDs or the girls from Gloucester on a Friday night.

Alec once told Rory he was mad for chasing after Amy for so long. 'Mate, there's a whole barrage of girls out there. Why waste time on the loony one?'

But Rory had always known Amy wasn't mad (well... OK, not *that* mad) and, despite the insult, Rory had been there for Alec throughout their teens. Throughout Mandy. And Claire. And Nazeem. And even Tess.

Then, aged 19, Alec's car had come off the slip road from Junction 8. The police said he'd been going way too fast, but at least he'd not been drinking. And for three weeks he'd been in ICU, and Rory had been one of the first people to speak to him when he woke up, and he'd been the person who'd called Alec's mum and dad and made sure they came to see him, and he'd been their point of contact over the next couple of weeks as they visited each evening.

So it had been Rory who had volunteered to tell them when they arrived one night, chocolates and magazines in hand, that Alec had had a massive heart attack an hour earlier. That his body wasn't strong enough. That it had been instantaneous. It was probably the bravest thing Rory had ever done up to that point in his life. Volunteering to face that grief, that shock. To hold Alec's mum as she cried. To take them both in to say goodbye.

Then there'd been the cremation, helping them choose music for the service. At the wake afterwards at the family house, he and Amy had gone out for air. Into the back garden.

God, that willow tree had looked so small and

insignificant then. It wasn't a flesh-eating monster any more. Or a spaceship or a truck or a cave or anything else it had been to two young boys, full of life and adventure. It was just a silly old tree that needed trimming back.

Rory had cried a lot that night. Whether it was just for Alec or for the realisation that childhood was gone for ever, he'd not been sure.

Amy had been great, too. Like she understood what it was to lose something that mattered when you were a kid.

He felt her now, her breath on his neck, her hand on his arm, as they both stared at Nathaniel Porter's willow tree.

'Yours made a better spaceship,' she whispered.

And that was why he loved Amy so much. She knew. She understood. They understood one another so well.

The reverie was broken as the dining room door was pushed open by the manservant, who was pushing a man in a wicker wheelchair. The man looked about 35 at most, Rory thought, but his hair was prematurely grey. Shockingly so. People talked about hair going grey overnight, but it rarely did. There were always a few strands of black or brown in there. But this guy looked like he'd had it dyed grey. Not an attractive silver but a dull, sheen-less grey.

His face was… odd. Like there was nothing there, no expression, no life.

Which was weird, because he was actually quite alert and physical. He was moaning at the manservant, saying it was embarrassing to be in the chair.

'I can walk, you know,' he said sharply, by way of explanation to the time travellers as well, Rory suspected, as to the manservant.

'Oliver Marks, I presume,' said the Doctor, stepping forward and offering a hand. Rather than shake it, Oliver grabbed his arm and hauled himself up.

Rory's training kicked in, and he took Oliver's weight on the other side to the Doctor, and they slowly walked Oliver to the table.

The manservant eased the wicker wheelchair away and left the room without speaking again.

'Thank you,' Oliver said. 'But I could've coped.'

The Doctor stepped away. 'Then Rory and I apologise for assuming you couldn't.'

'Oh, you weren't to know,' said Oliver. 'I'm sure Nathaniel Porter has been filling your head with stories about me, how weak and useless and mad I am. Well I am none of those things.'

Amy took a seat beside him, making eye contact and smiling. 'Hi, I'm Amy, a pleasure to meet you, Mr Marks.'

Oliver stared at her maybe a beat longer than Rory would have liked, but it did the trick, and the man smiled. 'Sorry,' he said.

Rory and the Doctor sat at the table, the Doctor

passing food around to them all as he talked. 'So, Mr Marks, how come you know our host? I gather you live here? A whole wing to yourself.'

'It's hardly a wing, Doctor,' he said. 'Two rooms and a bathroom. But it's comfortable and he's generous to let me stay here despite... well, everything.'

Amy passed him some salad tongs. 'Everything?'

Oliver filled his plate. 'I'm a friend of Mrs Porter's. But he lets me stay anyway.'

'The archaeologist?' asked Rory.

'Oh no, not her,' Oliver said. 'Although bless Enola, she is very sweet. No, the first Mrs Porter.'

'Ah, her again.' The Doctor started tucking into his food. 'Blimey this is good.'

'Good cook, Mrs Stern,' Oliver agreed. 'Worth her weight. Not that Nathaniel Porter really appreciates her. Hardly ever eats. Half the time, I wonder if he only keeps the staff on for my benefit.'

'And what benefit is that?'

Oliver looked at the Doctor. 'I'm not well, for the most part. I have good days and bad days. Today, you're seeing me on one of my good days.'

'That's very self-aware of you, Mr Marks,' the Doctor said.

'Call me Olly, please. It's my name. At least it was, until I started living here. Then it was "Mr Marks" this and "sir" that. Drives me bonkers. Or would, if I wasn't there already.'

'You don't seem bonkers to us,' said Amy.

Oliver laughed. 'As I say, a good day, so far. But rest assured, I'm not well.' He looked at the Doctor. 'I smell things, you see.'

'Really? Like what?'

But Rory cut in with a different question. 'How old are you, Olly?'

'Thirty-seven.'

Rory nodded. 'I see. When did you start smelling things?'

Oliver didn't answer. He just shot Rory a look as though he hadn't understood the question, and carried on eating.

The Doctor started to ask something else, but Rory tapped his forearm and shook his head. The Doctor looked quizzically at Rory for a second then back to Oliver and changed the subject. 'We're here to investigate the dig. Lots of complaints. We're from the Ministry.'

Oliver shrugged. 'I don't hear complaints,' he said. 'Mind you, can't remember the last time I went into the village. Can't imagine why anyone would complain though. Schools are on holiday, most of the village is away.'

'Away?'

'Yes, apparently in the summertime, the villagers often go away. Been away for a long time… I think. But at least there's less noise out there. I… I notice noise, you see.'

The Doctor gave Amy and Rory a *told you so*

look. 'Unusual for a village to empty itself though,' he pushed on.

Oliver shrugged. 'May be to do with the dig. Knowing Nathaniel Porter, he probably paid for them all to clear out. Just the farmers and a few shops left, I should think.'

The Doctor popped a piece of cold ham into his mouth. 'Wonder how Mrs Stern gets her fresh produce if the villagers are all away.'

Oliver tapped his plate with his fork. 'Cold store, in the basement. Keeps it fresh for months.'

'In 1936? I don't think so,' said the Doctor and got his sonic screwdriver out, and activated it, trying to get readings of some sort.

Amy looked quizzically at him as the little device screeched away to itself, and the Doctor muttered. 'Hmm, no alien tech registering. But then, maybe I need to be in the basement.'

Rory was still watching Oliver Marks. He had stopped eating. He was staring straight ahead, apparently at a bowl of salad.

Except he wasn't really, Rory could see that. He was just… staring. And his hands were rigid, like claws. His whole body had stopped.

'Turn it off, Doctor,' Rory hissed.

The Doctor looked affronted, but when he saw Oliver he switched off the sonic. 'Oliver?'

No response.

'What's up with him?' Amy wondered, but Rory shushed her, got up and went to Oliver's side.

Very quietly, he spoke. 'Oliver, when you said you could smell things, what did you mean?'

No response.

'Are you with me, Oliver?' Rory continued. 'Oliver, what are you smelling right now?'

Oliver opened his mouth to speak, but nothing came out at first. Then finally he spoke. 'I can smell them.'

'Who are "them"?'

Oliver flattened his hands on the table top. 'I can hear them, too. Through the vibrations. I can hear screaming. Smell gas. And fire. So much fire...'

'He can smell burning, Doctor,' Amy hissed. 'Is this place on fire?'

'Please, Amy,' Rory said. 'He can't smell burning, he can smell fire. It's different.'

The Doctor nodded. 'Of course.'

'Oh great,' muttered Amy. 'I'll sit back and wait to be told what's going on.'

Oliver's hands had relaxed, but he was sweating badly, shaking a little. He looked at Rory, as if realising he was crouched beside him for the first time. 'They're coming back, you know,' he said. 'Coming for me!'

Before anyone could speak, the door opened and Nathaniel Porter strode in, followed by Chuggers, or whatever he was really called, and another man, much older, with a pronounced limp.

'We'll take care of Mr Marks,' the manservant said, almost shoving the wheelchair towards him, as the limping man got Oliver up. Oliver didn't resist or anything, he just allowed the two men to put him into the chair and wheel him away.

'Now hang on—' Rory started, but the Doctor intervened.

'Will he be all right?' he asked Nathaniel Porter.

Their host nodded. 'My staff will look after him, he'll be fine after a little sleep.'

'You drug him?' asked Rory.

'Usually. It's why he has the wheelchair – they keep him tired and exhausted, so the chair is a safer option than walking.'

'What's wrong with him?' Amy asked.

Nathaniel Porter looked at them. 'My friend is… unwell. It was why the first Mrs Porter had him brought here. Their families were old friends. After my wife… disappeared, I still felt I had a duty to care for him.' He went to the door. 'Forgive my manners, but I wish to check that he is comfortable.'

And he was gone.

'Welcome to the Addams Family and the Munsters all rolled into one,' said Amy.

'Rory, what do you think?'

'Sorry?'

'You're the nurse, you're our expert, I need to know your thoughts.'

Rory was surprised – the Doctor had never actually sought his opinion on much before. 'God if this is the 1930s, they'll be using psychotropics and sedatives on him because they haven't got a clue what they're dealing with! He's suffering badly from PTSD.'

'Come again,' said Amy.

'Post-Traumatic Stress Disorder,' the Doctor said. 'He's mid-thirties, would have been early twenties in the war, so he could have shellshock.' He looked back at Rory and Amy. 'Back then PTSD hadn't been diagnosed, so they called it shellshock. Their treatment of it and its sufferers was not a particularly proud moment in mankind's history.'

'It's more than that, Doctor,' said Rory. 'People with PTSD often exhibit the signs that we saw then. It's called heightened sensory perception – they can smell or hear things associated with the trauma, usually things that most people can't normally smell or hear. The way he put his hands flat on the table, he was feeling vibrations. Tiny ones we'll never feel, but when he has a… a moment, everything is ramped up really high. The tiniest things can set him off.'

'My screwdriver?'

'Either the noise, or the green light, but when you activated it, it flicked a switch on in him, too.'

'But what in the sonic could make him remember the war?' Amy wondered. 'Is that what made him prematurely grey?'

'Diffuse alopecia areata is rare,' Rory said, 'and frankly a bit of a myth in the sense that shock doesn't really turn the hair grey. Not even in the First World War.'

'I don't think it's the war,' said the Doctor. 'Not entirely. Although that might account for the nerves. No, he said "They" were coming.'

'And that he could hear and smell them.'

'I thought he could smell fire,' said Amy. 'So if he doesn't mean burning, are you saying his senses have been changed enough to do that?'

Rory shook his head. 'We know so little about PTSD, it's tragic, even in our time, Amy. Different people react to different treatments because every case is, well, different. We had a few local soldiers come to the hospital after being in Afghanistan and Iraq, and some of them showed signs of PTSD, sometimes really powerfully, others just traces.'

Amy touched Rory's arm. 'You never talked about it. I had no idea you'd had people like that to deal with.'

'We didn't really talk about my work that much, did we Amy,' Rory said. Not unkindly, just stating a matter of fact. 'After the Atraxi and escaped Prisoner Zeros, I didn't really want to bother you with what I got up to every day at work. The hospital wasn't somewhere I thought you'd really want to keep visiting after what happened to you there.' He smiled at her. 'And it was quite nice to be able to go out in the evenings and weekends with you and not talk about work. I appreciated that.'

'I wonder who 'they' are, though,' said the Doctor, bringing them back to the subject in hand. 'If Olly's PTSD enables him to sense someone or something, we need to know what it is.'

'And he *can* sense them, Doctor. I can't explain how exactly, but it's very real and dangerous to people like Oliver. And fire is one of the strongest triggers out there – there are cases of people smelling a bonfire three miles away or if they were affected by gunfire, hearing thunder ten minutes before everyone else.' Rory headed to the door. 'They don't have a clue in 1936 what they are dealing with, or how fragile Oliver is. I ought to go and see him, check up on him.'

The Doctor shook his head. 'No, no, I can entertain Olly for a while. Amy, go and see your new special friend Tom – ah ah ah, shut up, Rory – find out a bit more about village life and how much it's changed over the last few years.'

'How do we know it has? Olly just said it was quiet, but he doesn't get out much.'

The Doctor smiled at her. 'Yes, but the first Mrs Porter is our clue here. I bet everything was fine until she died, vanished, fell into a deep hole, took a trip in a Gemini spaceship, whatever. Let's find out.' He winked at Rory. 'And you, my walking medical encyclopaedia, need to head to the library and research everything you can about the history of this village. Because if the new Mrs Porter is going to dig something up in the schoolyard, I'd like a clue as to what it might be.'

'I trust you enjoyed your lunch,' said Nathaniel Porter, suddenly in the room with them.

'Oh yes,' said the Doctor. 'It was the best cold meat salad I've ever had in 1936. Compliments to Mrs S and her kitchen. So simple, yet so brilliant. Much like Rory here.'

Nathaniel Porter waved expansively. 'My home is your home, Doctor. All three of you must come and go as you see fit. I would hate you to ever think you are imposing, because you are not.' He clicked his fingers and the old man with the limp hobbled in. 'Old John here will be your personal aide during your stay.'

Old John looked anything but pleased with this arrangement but said nothing.

'Splendid.' The Doctor held his hand out to Old John. 'Hullo, dear, we've not been properly introduced. I'm the Doctor, that's Amy Pond, that's Rory Williams, and you've been here a very long time, haven't you? Splendid, I like a man with a history and a firm handshake.' He threw a look at Nathaniel Porter. 'Can tell a lot by a handshake. We're here to help sort out the problem with the dig. I gather the locals are up in arms. Are you? Up in arms, I mean. Because you look the kind of fellow who doesn't get up in arms about very much, which makes you my new best friend…'

The Doctor was still gabbling as he led Old John down the dark corridor towards the hallway, leaving Amy and Rory looking at one another.

'Library?' said Rory.

'Sexy farmhand,' said Amy. 'I get the better

deal.'

They turned to ask Nathaniel Porter about their respective missions and how best to achieve them, but the dining room was now empty.

'Where did he go?' Amy wondered.

Old John led the Doctor back to the hallway and to the front door.

'We have put Mr Oliver out in the rear garden, Doctor,' he said quietly. 'He likes to grow a few flowers. Keeps him... calm.'

The Doctor regarded Old John carefully. 'You don't much like it here, do you, John? Is it Mr John, or is John your first name?'

'Just call me Old John, sir.'

'No thanks. Sounds rude. How long have you worked here, John?'

'For ever, sir.'

The Doctor regarded the old man carefully. 'I know what you mean.' He followed him out into the warm summer afternoon. 'How did Oliver Marks end up here? At the Manse?'

'Something bad happened to him, sir,' said Old John. 'Mrs Porter, the proper one, took him in. Friend of friends I believe. Not my place to ask, sir, you see.' He pointed at the impressive flowerbeds that lay curiously overgrown or barren. 'I was the gardener, see. Then, after Mrs Porter disappeared all sudden, like, I had a small accident and ended up retiring from the garden. Mr Nathaniel was kind enough to keep me on to help with Mr Oliver.'

The Doctor nodded sagely. 'You are a man of contradictions, John.'

'How's that, sir?'

'You work for a man you clearly don't like, who has married a wife you clearly don't approve of, and you've given up a job you clearly loved but stayed here to look after a man you barely know.'

Old John looked at the Doctor as if challenging him. Just for a moment, but it was enough to make the Doctor smile. 'I'll thank you, sir, not to judge me,' Old John said.

'Oh, John, I'm not judging. Certainly not. Observing maybe. You look after Olly because he's your last link to the first Mrs Porter. You stay here because you believe one day she'll be back to make sense of all this confusion.' He patted Old John's shoulder. 'I admire loyalty. And hope. And that little bit of stupidity necessary to make both of them achievable in this modern world.' He pointed to the corner of the Manse, where Oliver Marks was sat in his wicker wheelchair, leaning forward, pruning some roses. 'And that man needs your help, John. Yours and mine, am I right?'

'Maybe. Especially after the rest of the villagers started leaving.'

'Fairly normal, even now. Picture-postcard English villages are dying out, people moving to towns and cities for work, post-Depression.'

'It's not that, sir. People just started going

overnight, like they couldn't get away fast enough. Some stayed of course, as you've seen, loyal to the old family.'

'The Porters?'

'Been in charge of Shalford Heights since the thirteenth century. So they say.'

'Goes some way to explaining the lack of cricket on the green, people in the pub and why no one's ever built a church.'

'Oh there was one. Burned to the ground about twenty years ago. A small one, more a chapel really.'

And no one rebuilt it? That's... unheard of.'

'Mr Porter always said he planned to, but after the first Mrs Porter's death he just gave up on it. Maybe that is a reason why people moved away.'

'Maybe. Maybe not.' The Doctor suddenly grabbed Old John's wrist, pulling his rough jacket up a bit, exposing the old man's wrist. 'Now I may not know much about the British social mores of the 1930s, but I'm willing to bet that a man wearing a leather bracelet-strap-bangle thing like that, especially with those little tassely bits and the beads, well I bet that's not very manly and popular down the Nag's Head is it?'

Old John pulled his wrist away, covering the strap. 'If it's all the same to you now, sir, I need to go and prepare Mr Oliver's set of rooms. He likes a nap just after lunch.'

'He hasn't had any lunch, John. He had one of his

moments, as well you know. How did you know, by the way?'

'Mr Nathaniel told me.'

'And I wonder how he knew.' The Doctor smiled and gave Old John a little bow. 'Fine. Thank you, John. You have been most helpful.' And he stared at the old man until he shuffled off. Then, just as he was about to disappear from view, back towards the main door of the Manse, the Doctor called after him. 'Oh, John?'

'Sir?'

'I am on your side, you know,' the Doctor said quietly, but loud enough for Old John to hear. 'Always. Remember that.'

Old John touched his wrist, the one with the leather band on it. 'I hope so,' he said enigmatically and wandered away.

The Doctor smiled to himself. 'Top man, that,' he muttered, then turned to Oliver Marks.

'Nice flowers, Olly,' he said so loudly people in the village could probably hear. 'Quite the horticulturalist, aren't you.'

Oliver Marks put the flowers down and reached forward, grabbing the Doctor's arms. He pulled him right down, so the Doctor's face was level with his own. Unnaturally close. 'You can feel it too, can't you?'

The Doctor frowned but didn't pull away. 'Feel what, Oliver?'

'Them. They are coming. Touch the ground. Feel

their approach. They are always coming, but now they are so close.' He gasped, almost as if it pained him just to speak like this. 'They killed everyone.'

'The Germans?'

'No!' Oliver yelled that. Then, back to normal, he said, 'I thought you'd understand. They're not human. They came. Killed everyone. Burned them to nothing. Can't you smell them?'

'Who, Oliver? Tell me who.'

'I don't know their names. They burned the people, the houses, the dogs and cats, the trees, the grass. They burned Daisy.'

The Doctor picked up the roses. 'Daisies. Is that why you like the flowers, Oliver? Because they destroyed the flowers?'

'Daisy is my fiancée. Was my fiancée!'

The Doctor closed his eyes in annoyance. At himself. How stupid. Of course Daisy was a person, not a flower.

'I shut my eyes, I see her screaming. I go to sleep, I see them in my dreams. Destroying everything in Little Cadthorpe. And now they're coming back. For me. To finish me off because I saw them.' Oliver suddenly started crying.

The Doctor stood up, patting Oliver awkwardly on the shoulder. 'BRB, Olly.'

Oliver looked up through red-ringed eyes, uncomprehendingly.

'Sorry – be right back,' the Doctor translated and headed back inside the Manse. 'Phone, phone,

phone – saw a marvellous old Ericsson in the hallway earlier,' he muttered to himself.

Yes, there it was: black Bakelite, on a table by the doorway to the kitchen.

'Top of the range for 1936, Nathaniel Porter, good on you.'

He got out his sonic screwdriver and traced the wire to a small black box on the wall. He zapped the box and then the actual cord all the way back to the phone itself. 'Hope this works, Doctor. Only get one chance with these old phones.' He returned the sonic screwdriver to his jacket pocket (but not before twirling it like a majorette's baton a couple of times) and then lifted the receiver off the cradle. Using the old circular fascia, he dialled a number. It rang. 'Oh, Doctor, you are good,' he said to himself.

After a few seconds it was answered. 'Rory, it's me,' he started. 'Yes, yes I know. Yes, OK so you shouldn't get a signal in 1936. No, no, you're right it is impossible. However, I'm talking and you're listening. Well except you're not, because you're talking. As usual. Will. You. Just. Listen?' A beat. 'Oh, oh right, yes, you are listening. OK, you at the Library yet? Well, why not?' Another beat. 'Oh Rory, she's getting information from him, that's all. You so have to get over this jealous streak, it's very unattractive. Well, to Amy, actually, but I suppose I also find it unattractive, yes. En. Ee. Way – can you look up anything about a village called Little Cadthorpe. No, I don't, but it sounds English. It's where I think Oliver Marks was traumatised. Yes, you were right, it wasn't the war… No, I am not being patronising. OK I *am* being patronising but sometimes you… never mind. What?' The Doctor sighed. 'OK. Please. Thank you. No, actually, I could take you to a couple of planets where it costs a great deal actually. No, clearly I'm not going to take you there, I'd be bankrupt on your behalf in minutes.'

He hung up and went back outside to Oliver Marks and his roses.

Chapter
6

In the school library which, he suspected, doubled as a library for the whole village if not further afield, Rory was flicking through an oversized book of newspapers when there was a gentle cough behind him. It wasn't the cough of someone who was ill, or even clearing their throat. No, this was that worldwide-accepted cough of someone who wanted to attract your attention but was too embarrassed to ask.

Rory smiled to himself and imagined what the Doctor would do. No doubt he'd oh so politely charm the newcomer, offer them a seat beside him and smile a lot, flatter them by doing that thing he did so well – staring them straight in the eyes, making them believe that, at that precise moment in space and time, they were the only person in the world who mattered. That the rest of the universe could go to hell, because the only person whose thoughts/opinions/feelings that mattered was them.

Rory knew this because he'd been the subject of it many times. Well, he thought, actually 'victim' was probably a better word. Well, he said victim, but that sounded too cruel, too... malicious, and the Doctor was many things but malicious, cruel and unpleasant wasn't one of them. Three of them. Whatever.

'How can I help you?' he said, turning on his Doctor-charm-offensive mode as best he could. Unfortunately, he forgot he was holding the big book of newspapers and whacked it into the cougher's midriff. Which was quite a large target as it turned out, and the lady concerned seemed a bit taken aback to have been assaulted in such a manner by a man she'd never met.

Rory couldn't blame her for this, especially as the earthenware mug she'd been carrying hit the ground with enough force to shatter into fragments. 'Oh my God,' he gasped. 'Oh my God, I'm so sorry.'

The rather... rotund lady held her tummy with one hand and started waving the other, wheezing something that was probably meant to be 'It's all right young man, accidents happen,' but instead came out as a series of rasping grunts.

'Your poor mug,' was Rory's next attempt at a platitude, but the foreboding look he got found him flushing bright red.

The lady finally composed herself and dropped, rather more elegantly than Rory would have suspected possible, to one knee to begin picking up the remnants of the smashed mug. When she had finished, she balled the bits in her fist and held it out to Rory. 'Bin,' she said. 'Under your table.'

'Bin? Oh right, bin, yes, absolutely.' He reached down, found a straw wastepaper bin and held it up.

The woman deposited the results of his clumsiness in the bin. 'You must be with the dig,' she said as she hauled herself up. 'Nancy Thirman,' she added, sticking out a damp, tea-stained hand.

Fearing further upset, Rory quickly shook it. The woman had a powerful shake, like a man's. Or a woman used to having to be strong and determined in a man's world.

'Good to have you in the village,' she added. 'Don't give a hoot what others might say.'

'Others?' Rory thought this was interesting.

'Yes, ruddy naysayers from the WI. Ignore the blighters, that's what I say. Now, other than bring you fresh tea, as I seem to be wearing your last one, what can I get you?'

Rory frowned.

'I'm the librarian, schoolteacher, former munitions worker and all-round good egg, even if I say so myself. And I do because, as sure as heck, no one else will. Not these days.' She tapped the big newspaper book Rory had just coshed her with. 'Good tome, if you want the official, sanitised version of stuff. Bit rubbish, of course, if you want the truth about the village.'

'The truth?'

'That's why you're here, isn't it? Don't want to read all that stuff and nonsense. You need the real history.' Nancy tapped her head. 'All in here. The truth. About the Porters.'

Rory gaped. He knew he wanted to know about the Porters, but how did she? Why would she even suspect? It crossed Rory's mind that maybe it was his fault – had he said something, done something, looked at something in the wrong way that had revealed his 'mission'? No, that was daft. He might not have been at the game for long but he'd gleaned enough from the Doctor and Amy not to make mistakes like that. Again.

Nancy was smiling broadly now. 'Oh, I know things, you see. It's my job to know things. Like what you are thinking right now. And I'll tell you this. I knew Mrs Porter. We were at Roedean together. Grew up. Inseparable. Till she met Nathaniel Porter.'

'You were at school with Enola Porter?' Rory thought that was unlikely – Nancy was 60 if she was a day.

'Oh, not her,' Nancy snorted. 'Not that I had a problem with her. No I mean the real Mrs Porter. Who vanished.' Nancy turned and left, muttering something about making fresh tea.

Rory went back to his book, energised. So the first Mrs Porter hadn't just died, she'd actually vanished. Even her best friend didn't know what had really happened.

'Bet you didn't know that, Doctor Smug-Pants,' he grunted as he turned the pages. His attention was no longer focused on Enola but on finding out about the other one. Whose name he'd forgotten to ask.

Rory flicked through page after page, but slowly began to wonder if Nancy Thirman was a bit… mad. Because there were no references in anything he read that suggested the first Mrs Porter had vanished. In fact, disappointingly, there were no references to her at all.

The wife of the local bigwig? Seemed unlikely.

Even the wedding report on when Porter had married Enola Tucker made no reference to him being married before.

Rory remembered the Doctor's request about Little Cadthorpe. He found a few references. Apparently, a fire at a flourmill had spread through the village one night. The reports weren't gruesome, but the details were certainly heartrending. Lists of names after a tragedy always upset Rory. So many names. Some were entire families, wiped out in one go. Always upsetting.

A whole village, gone up in smoke overnight. No survivors.

Mind you, that was odd. Even in the worst disasters, it was pretty remarkable if no one survived. Someone would surely have escaped or gone to get help.

Then Rory remembered: Oliver Marks had been there, and he had escaped. So why did none of the reports make mention of that? He closed the big book and carried it back to the shelf it had come from, glancing over at the library clock.

Nancy Thirman had obviously given up on the tea – more than half an hour had passed since she'd wandered away.

Oh well, he'd get a cuppa back at the Manse.

He looked around the library. Nope, he was alone, no one else was there. Perhaps he ought to turn out the lights. This was 1936, and electricity was probably quite expensive.

'Hullo,' he called out. 'Miss Thirman? Shall I, you know, the lights? Off I mean? As you do?'

Nothing.

With a shrug, Rory moved towards the light, then he felt his foot tap something. Looking down, he saw it was a ball of green wool. Where on earth had that come from?

Rory was about to reach down when something stopped him. Just a feeling, a niggling thing at the back of his head, that same instinct you have not to touch a poisonous berry or a dog that might actually nip your ankles. He couldn't explain it, but he gently kicked the woollen ball away, watching it roll under a desk.

He wandered over to the lights and was reaching up when he felt something at his feet again.

It was that ball of green wool. It was an odd colour. Sort of sick or dead colour, a mix of greens and yellows combined to make one very unattractive shade. No one would want a Christmas sweater created in that wool, Rory was sure.

This time he gave it a hefty punt across the library, flicked off the lights and was gone.

As he left the big room, he passed by a small office, its light still on.

On the door was a name plaque: N THIRMAN, CUSTODIAN.

He eased the door open.

There was no sign of Nancy Thirman. What there was, however, was a massive hammock-like thing, suspended across the room. If that wasn't weird enough, it was made of wool. Like it was knitted. Knitted in the same sickly colour as the ball he'd seen in the library. Unlike a traditional hammock, Rory realised, this was solid – no way into it, so it looked more like a fat woollen runner bean pod.

No wonder there were balls of wool lying around – this had to have taken Nancy Thirman months to knit.

Oh well, each to their own.

He was about to leave when the hammock-pod-woollen thing suddenly quivered, swaying from side to side on the two woollen strands which connected it to the opposite walls. As Rory leaned in to stare, part of it seemed to grow, to move, like a woollen stump pushing out towards him. Then the end of it moved, like the wool was being knitted in front of his eyes, forming…. forming a face.

A woman's face. Eyes, nose, mouth, hair – like some hideous unfinished woollen toy, the face suddenly flexed, the mouth, still just made of wool, seemed to weave itself open in an open-mouthed grimace.

Rory recognised the face. He realised he was staring into a woollen facsimile of Nancy Thirman's face, twisted into tortured, silent fury.

As slowly as it had emerged, the face-on-a-stump was reabsorbed into the pod. Then, after a final quiver, the knitted pod hung still and silent.

Rory ran.

The Doctor was sniffing a pink rose on a very lush bush attached to a trellis that ran up the side of the Manse, on the same side of the building as Oliver's room. It veered slightly at one point to the left then carried on straight, basically weaving its way, as much as a wooden trellis can be said to weave, around the bedroom window.

'Odd place to put a trellis,' he said to Oliver. 'I mean, why not three foot thataway and then you wouldn't need to put a kink in it.'

Oliver shrugged from his wheelchair and pulled his blanket closer to his waist but said nothing.

The Doctor carried on examining the plant architecture, wandering around the corner, carefully not treading on any of the flowerbeds, but counting bricks to himself.

'What do you remember of that day, Oliver?' he called out after a few minutes.

'What day?'

'Oh, you know what day,' the Doctor replied. 'Unless you don't want to talk about it.'

'Not much.' Oliver tried to press himself further into the wheelchair, as if that would make him feel safe from the Doctor's sudden probing. 'I try not to think about it.' He gripped the blanket again, as if trying to stop it falling to the ground, even though there was little chance of that.

'Fair enough. I understand completely. Not talking. Good move. Talking is so overrated.' The Doctor began tapping on the window to Oliver's bedroom. 'Dunno why people spend so much time talking. Communication. Pointless exercise, I always say. Well, I say "always"... I mean "sometimes". Well, no, actually I don't mean "sometimes", I actually mean never, cos communication is really important, and I like communicating with people.' He popped his head back around the corner and winked at Oliver. 'But no pressure,' he said and darted away again.

Oliver sighed and was about to say something but stopped.

Finally, he spoke. 'Gas. Petroleum. Fire.'

The Doctor's head bobbed back into view. 'What's up, Olly? Oh.'

The Doctor stopped for the same reason that Oliver had started.

A woman was standing next to Oliver. Very close.

Oliver Marks was staring at her in shock.

The Doctor frowned, trying to work out what was wrong with this picture. But he couldn't figure it out so instead just said a simple 'Can we help you?' to the woman.

She held herself well, very prim and proper, regarding the Doctor carefully, head slightly tilted to one side. She was dressed in a simple dress and coat, her hair bobbed slightly.

'No,' she said.

The Doctor smiled at her and walked forward, offering his hand. 'Hullo. I don't believe I've had the pleasure.'

The woman ignored the hand.

Oliver also tried to reach out to her, but she stepped behind his chair. In doing so, she drew the Doctor's gaze away from the building and back towards the long drive and the village beyond.

The Doctor frowned – pelting down the driveway towards them was Rory. He slowed as he got closer, nodding an unreturned greeting to the new woman as he moved in front of her to address the Doctor.

'Weird thing,' he panted, trying to catch his breath. 'Really, really weird.'

The Doctor reached out with both arms and eased Rory out of his line of vision, but there was now only Oliver Marks, slumped in his wheelchair, hugging his blanket to his chest, as if affected by a sudden, powerful chill, despite the warmth of the afternoon.

The woman had gone. Completely. Presumably into the Manse – there was nowhere else for her to have gone so quickly.

'I need to follow that woman,' the Doctor said to Rory and walked, very quickly, away, reaching out to casually pat Oliver's shoulder as he passed. 'Rory, look after Olly, please,' he called back.

'But what about…' Rory began. But it was no use; the Doctor was ignoring him. 'What about Nancy Thirman?' he finished rather lamely to himself.

Then he felt a hand on his, gripping tightly – too tightly, in fact – and he knelt down and slowly unclasped Oliver's hand from his. 'It's all right, Mr Marks,' he said in his best nurse's tone. 'Everything's going to be fine. If it's the drugs that are making you feel woozy, that'll be why Nathaniel Porter needs to keep you in the chair.'

'No it isn't,' Oliver snapped, still clutching the blanket. 'They're coming. I can feel it. Everywhere.'

'I need you to try and tell me about it. As much as you can bear to,' Rory said.

Oliver shook his head. 'Can't. Can't talk about it.' He looked Rory straight in the eyes. 'I'm very sorry.'

Rory didn't know what Oliver Marks was sorry for, but he could see he really meant it. He watched a single tear trickle down Oliver's face.

Despite the warm summer afternoon air that had settled in a comfortable haze over the whole village and the nice glow of the sunshine, Rory suddenly felt bitterly cold. It was as if someone hadn't just walked over his grave this time; they'd driven a sixteen-tonne artic over it.

'They're coming back, and this time they'll get me,' said Oliver.

'Why d'you say that then?'

'Because she's here. Again. She's back.'

'Who? That lady the Doctor's gone to find?'

Oliver nodded slowly.

'Who is she?' asked Rory.

Oliver was looking down now at his blanket, tracing its pattern with a trembling finger. 'My fiancée.'

For a not especially large house, the Manse was quite labyrinthine in its layout, the Doctor thought. He stood in the Manse hallway at the apex of the three inner corridors. Each led in a different direction, and the mysterious woman could have taken any of them.

'Eeny meeny, miny, but no mo,' he muttered, ticking off each one. 'Or she could've taken the stairs,' the Doctor supposed looking up at the huge wooden staircase that led to the upper storey. 'Hey, steps, you can be Mo if you want?'

The staircase didn't answer.

'Be like that then,' he muttered. 'I'm going with Eeny.'

He headed towards Oliver's room at the back of the house, trying to ignore the creaky, noisy wooden flooring beneath his boots. Stealth wasn't exactly an option.

'1936,' he murmured. 'You'd think it was 1836. Thomas Edison would be so disappointed that his discovery wasn't being used here.' He tapped a nearby light fitting that wasn't illuminated, and looked for a switch. Not finding one, he brought out his sonic screwdriver and zapped the light bulb. It glowed brightly, casting eerie shadows across the long wood-panelled corridor. Another light bulb, another zap, and the shadows melted away. 'That's more comfortable,' the Doctor said.

'If it's light you require, Doctor, God's own light bulb is outside.'

The Doctor turned to find Nathaniel Porter behind him. Quite how he'd got there without the Doctor hearing him was a mystery, but he was there.

'I'm looking for a lady,' the Doctor explained, raising a hand. 'Yay high, nice coat, bit austere. I think she came in here.'

'Into my house? Uninvited? That seems unlikely.' Nathaniel Porter smiled. 'I don't let any old riff-raff in here, do I, Doctor?'

The Doctor smiled at Porter's dig. 'I can't think where else she might have gone,' he said. 'Unless you can shed any light on it?'

Nathaniel Porter glanced at the newly lit bulbs but resisted rising to the Doctor's pun. 'I seriously doubt any lady has come here, Doctor.'

'She was outside. I spoke to her.' He stared closely at Nathaniel Porter. 'She was standing next to Mr Marks. He seemed rather... perturbed by this.' The Doctor saw a flicker of... doubt? Consternation? Certainly something crossed the man's face, but the Doctor couldn't quite read what.

'I tell you, Doctor, no one has entered my house bar your good self. And I am not convinced that Mr Marks would be entirely comfortable with you... prowling around his rooms.'

'Oh, are they down here? I had no idea. I was looking for the kitchen. Fancied a bit of food. A cake? Scone? Shortbread? Love shortbread. Why's it called shortbread, though? Neither short nor a bread.'

Nathaniel Porter shrugged. 'I thought you were looking for a lady.' He pointed back along the passage to the main hall. 'The kitchen is that way. But I believe you know that already.'

The Doctor looked hard at Nathaniel Porter. 'Something strange is going on in Shalford Heights. I'm not sure if you're unaware of it, ignoring it, or right at the heart of it.' The Doctor adjusted his bow tie as if that was some recognisable gesture of defiance. 'But I'm pretty sure that I'll find out over the next day or so.'

Nathaniel Porter suddenly bellowed with laughter. 'What a funny young man you are,' he said. 'In my house, in my village, and you are threatening me. I'm not sure whether to be flattered, amused or insulted. Right now, I choose to be amused.' And the laughter stopped as suddenly as it had begun. Nathaniel Porter, however, continued speaking. 'Be very sure, Doctor, that it does not turn to "insulted", because if it does you and your friends will no longer be welcome here. And Shalford Heights can be as unfriendly and uninviting as it needs to be.'

'As it needs to be? Or as you need it to be?'

Nathaniel Porter again pointed back to the main hallway. 'My dear Doctor,' he said quietly. 'As I'm sure you have realised, that is one and the same thing.'

The Doctor sidled past Porter, zapped the light bulbs off, pocketed the sonic screwdriver and began walking back to the hallway, defeated in his investigations. For now.

'Oh, Doctor, one last thing.'

The Doctor threw him an enquiring look.

'Tell me, where is your friend Amelia Pond? I haven't seen her in a while.' Nathaniel Porter smiled a smile that never reached his eyes. 'You don't want her wandering off again, do you?'

The Doctor held his gaze for a second and then turned and left and walked slowly back up the corridor till he got to a turn, then looked back, saying, 'That had better not be a threat…' He trailed off – the corridor behind him was empty. Like the mysterious woman that had brought him into the Manse in the first place, Nathaniel Porter had just melted into the shadows and vanished.

Something told the Doctor that if he retraced his steps, Nathaniel Porter would just as mysteriously return and shoo him out of his home. So he went straight out of the front door and back round to the side garden to find Oliver Marks and Rory Williams.

Who, of course, weren't there.

'I hate this place,' the Doctor muttered.

'I love this place,' said Tom Benson to Amy. 'I mean, who wouldn't. Sunshine, quiet, that smell of the countryside.'

'Pooh,' said Amy, sniffing.

'Sorry?'

'That's pooh. The smell of the countryside. Horses, cows, sheep. All the same. Pooh.'

Tom looked affronted and looked down at the small brook they were stood beside, which ran down one end of the village, the furthest from the Manse. Behind them, Shalford Heights was only a couple of minutes walk, but Amy could already tell the difference in atmosphere. Literally. The air was… different. It was as if she and Tom had walked out of a building and into the open air rather than just crossing a few roads.

And Amy had been travelling with the Doctor long enough now to trust her instincts – if something felt wrong, nine times out of ten, it was.

So why did Shalford Heights make her feel... queasy?

She hooked her arm around Tom's and smiled at him. 'Oh, sorry, I wasn't trying to upset you. I love the countryside. And I love it more now that you're showing it to me.'

'What's Scotland like?' he asked.

Amy shrugged. 'Been a long time since I was there. I think...' She was about to say something about Scotland but couldn't bring thoughts or words to her mind, so she changed the subject. 'I've been in England so long now, I think of it as home,' she lied. Truth was, she thought of the TARDIS as home more these days. Which wouldn't be a popular thought to vocalise in front of Rory, she decided.

Then, knowing Rory, he'd have something to say about her being here with Tom. Poor Rory – thrust into the Doctor's mad life of universal criminals, alien vampires, strange nightmares and now this. Mind you, she had to admit, he was throwing himself into it with vigour and positivity – and she smiled at that thought. God bless Rory.

Tom eased his arm away from Amy. 'You're thinking about him, aren't you?'

She looked at Tom in surprise. 'I'm sorry?'

'Your boyfriend. Fiancé. Whatever he is.'

Amy opened her mouth to answer but no words came out.

'It's all right,' Tom said. 'I'm not surprised. He's very… dynamic. A city type, probably rich.'

'Not really…'

'And really clever,' Tom carried on. 'I saw the way he looked around the village, taking it all in. I may not be clever, Miss Pond, but I can spot those that are. I hope you'll be very happy.'

'Well, I hope so, too. I think.'

'But you have to get that stupid bow tie off him. Even in the countryside we think they're old-fashioned.'

'Bow… Oh my God!' Amy roared with laughter. 'You think I'm engaged to the Doctor?'

'But you said he was your fiancé…'

'Not the Doctor! Rory! I'm marrying Rory!'

Tom stared at her. For quite a long time. Speechless. Then: 'Why?'

Amy frowned. 'Cos I love him. I think. No. Yeah, yeah, I do.'

'Rory? Not the Doctor? You're getting married to Rory?'

'Uh-huh.'

'Not. The. Doctor?'

'Nope, not the Doctor. Just friends. Mates. Pals.'

'Oh.' Tom picked a pebble up and tossed it into the brook. 'Oh,' he said again.

'Maybe we need to get back to the village,' Amy suggested, thinking the oppressive atmosphere in the village itself was preferable to the awkwardness of this conversation.

'There's something I wanted to show you first,' Tom said. 'Just over the other side of the brook. Mind getting your toes wet?'

'Course not,' Amy said, pulling her trainers off. 'Lead on.'

Tom jumped nimbly over the brook, but it was a fraction too wide even for him and he was a little short of the bank when he landed, but he moved with the expertise of someone used to doing this and was on the bank, shaking water off his thick boots before it had time to soak in. He gasped.

'You all right?' asked Amy.

'I... I'm not fond of water.'

Amy mock-sighed at him. 'Then why'd you bring me all this way, farmer-boy?'

'Because, annoyingly, there's no other way to get here. You take care.'

Amy took it more slowly, allowing her naked feet to be covered with the brook, feeling the moving water swill around her ankles as she gently walked through it to the other side.

Tom slipped his coat and sweater off, passing the latter to her to use as a towel.

'I'm OK,' she said, but Tom insisted, pointing out that they'd be walking on shale and twigs and stuff that would hurt her soles.

'So you'll need your pretty shoes on.'

She used the woolly sweater to dry her feet. It

was a strange sensation, almost as if the wool was actually absorbing the water – her feet were dry in seconds.

'Thank you,' she said, passing the sweater back. Tom tied it around his waist and offered her a gentlemanly hand up. 'Why thank you, kind sir,' Amy said again, but with a slight bow and a smile.

Tom smiled for the first time in a few minutes. 'You are… unusual,' he said. 'Not like the other girls in the village.'

'Ah well, I'm more of a town girl myself,' Amy said. 'I was brought up in a village but couldn't wait to get out and about. Visiting friends. And… stuff.'

'Where did you go?'

'Oh, here and there. Somehow I always ended up back in the village, though. Funny that,' she added, more to herself. 'Until now. Now, I have this friend and he takes me all over the place.'

'That sounds like… fun,' Tom said and it briefly crossed Amy's mind that he'd had to think for a moment about the word 'fun'. Perhaps the inhabitants of Shalford Heights didn't do 'fun' in 1936.

1936.

Wow.

No matter how many places the Doctor took her (oh, and Rory) she still couldn't quite get her head around time travel as a concept.

'It's 1936,' she said out loud and then caught Tom's face. 'Whoops. Of course it is, 1936. Same as it was yesterday.'

Tom was still staring at her curiously.

'Oh don't mind me, sexy boy. I just … say things sometimes. Silly things. Like dates. I like dates. I mean, I like date dates, like times and, um, dates. Not going on dates. Because, you know, I have Rory, so dating, waaaay back in the past. Oh look, another reference to dates. The time kind. I'll be quiet now.'

Tom just nodded slowly.

'Oh and I can't stand the fruits. Dates. Horrible bitter things. With giant pips in the middle. Stones – I mean why would you deliberately choose to eat something with stone at the centre? Especially when it tastes as bad as a date. Sooo, you had something you wanted to show me,' she added as fast as she could. 'Go on then, wow me.'

Quietly (nervously? If so, who could blame him), Tom led Amy into the woods and eventually to a small twisted clump of old trees, which had grown sideways rather than upright. It was a strange formation – there certainly didn't seem to be any real wind there that could cause this strange effect.

And they were an odd, but quite interesting, colour. A sort of greeny yellow that reminded her of dead things. The trees were fascinating. Almost…

'Beautiful,' Amy breathed. 'And quite amazing really. Did you find this place as a kid? Make it your den or something like that?'

Tom ignored her, reaching out to one of the tree forms and stroking its bark.

Except, Amy realised with a start, it wasn't bark. She wasn't immediately sure what it was, just that it wasn't tree bark. It looked like...

No.

No, that was silly.

But it did!

It looked like the trees were knitted. Out of wool.

Wool.

Like that stuff that you get from sheep.

Sheep wool.

Not all of them, she thought glancing around. Just these ones. These strangely formed, twisted ones. Made from wool.

'What do you think, Amy Pond?'

And then Tom did something so strange that Amy suspected he wasn't really called Tom Benson at all. Because his hand seemed to unravel, changing colour as it did so, becoming a sickly greeny-yellow-like-the-tree-bark-that-wasn't-bark-much. Unravelled! Like a ball of...

Oh.

Tom's arm was nearly gone now, flowing, thread by thread into the tree. Not round it, not over it but actually being absorbed by it. Then the whole right side of his body was going, although his head remained, balanced precariously on what ought to have been a lopsided shoulder with nothing to support it. Tom smiled at her.

'Well,' Amy said. 'That is certainly different.'

And then the tree reached out and grabbed her, and, not for the first time since she'd begun travelling with the Doctor, Amy blacked out.

Chapter
7

'Tell me what you saw, Oliver. All those months ago. I need to know everything.'

Rory and Oliver Marks were round the back of the willow tree, out of sight of the Manse and its many windows. Oliver had insisted upon this, so Rory had wheeled him here. Rory was kneeling beside the wicker wheelchair, holding Oliver's hand caringly. He repeated his request, explaining: 'The Doctor, me and Amy. We want to help you. If it helps, I saw something very weird at the library.'

Oliver slowly shook his head. 'No one needs to know everything, Rory. Some things are better left locked away. Up here.' He tapped the side of his forehead. 'For ever.'

Rory took Oliver's hand and squeezed it gently.

'I'm not going to try to pretend I can understand what you went through, or that I can feel it or share it. Because I can't. But I do know one thing.'

'What's that, then?'

'If you can't find a way to unlock it all, find a way to explain it to us, we have absolutely zero chance of stopping whatever it is that's going on here.'

'And this house, the whole of Shalford Heights and everyone in it will become a dim memory, blasted – quite literally – from history.' The Doctor was beside them suddenly, fingers steepled in front of his chin. 'Well, that might be an exaggeration, but then again, maybe it isn't.'

'When?' Oliver fidgeted uncomfortably. Like he knew something he wasn't telling them.

'Whenever the ball-of-wool monsters attack, I reckon,' said Rory.

Rory started to stand but Oliver wouldn't let go of his hand.

'Not them,' Oliver hissed. 'They're not the enemy.'

Rory eased his hand out of Oliver's frightened grip and stood up. He turned towards the Doctor, but Oliver grabbed his trouser leg with his right hand.

'They're coming,' announced Oliver. He had his left palms now wrapped around some of the willow branches and pulled them to his face and sniffed deeply. 'I can smell them on everything. Don't let them come back. For God's sake, don't let them come back…'

Rory tried to sound comforting. 'Why do you think that, Oliver?'

The Doctor was chewing his top lip. 'If Oliver says they're coming back, with his heightened senses, I'd risk quite a big wodge of cash that he's right. In which case, we need to know who he's talking about.' The Doctor clicked his fingers. 'Rory, wool. You said wool, he said not wool. Tell me about the wool.'

'Right. Yes. Got it. In the library, there was a lady, quite nice…'

'Oh, you dog, Rory, I thought you were a one-woman man!'

'She was 60, Doctor.'

'Oh. Sorry – carry on, nurse.'

Rory threw the Doctor a look, that said in no uncertain terms that he'd heard that one before. 'Anyway, she wasn't human, she was a big ball of wool, hanging in her office, like a hammock. Which is weird, but I'm telling you the truth.'

'Well of course you are.' The Doctor shrugged. 'Why wouldn't you be. Now, ball of wool. Aliens. Wool.' The Doctor spun around, punching his fist against his palm, as if trying to recall something. Then suddenly he stopped and pointed at Rory. 'Yes! Oh yes! Got it. The Weave, great race, lovely planet, fantastic barbecues.'

'Sounds dangerous.'

'Evolution, Rory. Can't set themselves on fire,

that'd send Darwin into a nervous breakdown if someone evolved that stupidly. Not fond of water though, takes for ever to de-soggify themselves. So – why are the Weave on Earth in 1936, and where are they?'

'In the library, I told you, pretending to be a librarian.'

'Did she give you a number?'

'What? Like a phone number? I told you, I wasn't trying to pick her up!'

'No, they don't have names, they have numbers. They are like one huuuuuuge family – each homestead, each business, each starship crew, like one big family, looking out for one another because their life cycle is sort of like a Fibonacci code. Each name, a successive number, added to the last. Literally. And each person exists to form a part of a greater whole. Remove one, and the Weave fall apart. Quite literally over time, I imagine.' The Doctor clapped his hands together. 'Yes, I remember now, I met a girl.'

'And I thought *I* was being accused of chatting them up.'

'Little girl, Rory. About 7 or 8 years old. This was about five or eight faces back...'

Oliver stared at the Doctor.

'Don't ask,' suggested Rory. 'I can't get my head around statements like that.'

The Doctor was still going. 'Took her for a spin around the cosmos, showed her the universe, got her home in time for tea. Gave her a homing beacon. Told her if ever she was in trouble to beep me, and I'd come get her.'

'And you think that's who was in the library?'

'Doubt it, she'd have said something to you. Did she say anything to you? About me, I mean?'

'No, all she went on about was the first Mrs Porter. Like she was trying to tell me something. Mind you, she was a bit odd because I threw tea all over her.'

'Got her soggy. Nice one, Rory. What did I tell you about the Weave?'

'Nothing till two minutes ago.'

'Oh. Yes, OK, not your fault you got her/him/it wet.'

'Whoa,' said Rory. 'Back up. Her/him/it?'

'The Weave aren't like your species. Humans – male, female, that's your basic range. The Weave are effectively asexual. They take on characteristics depending on their mood, what looks good aesthetically or what that particular family group want or need. When they take on another person's form, like your librarian, they copy the original but that doesn't mean that your woolly librarian was a female Weave originally.' He suddenly slapped his forehead. 'Of course. Nathaniel Porter. He must be one of them.'

Oliver Marks had been looking from one to the other, like watching a tennis match. Eventually he butted in. 'That wasn't who I saw.'

'No,' said the Doctor. 'Life wouldn't be that simple, would it. To echo Rory earlier, tell us everything.'

'I never have,' Oliver said. 'I... I can't. I try to lock it all away, Doctor. I picture a little box in my mind, with a lock and everything and I try to put the memories in there. But it's no use. In my head. In my dreams. Always replaying, over and over again. I think I'm going mad. No one understands.'

'Yes they do,' said Rory gently. 'Maybe not here, maybe not in 1936, but where I come from, we're beginning to. You're ill, but you're certainly not mad. It's all because of whatever you experienced in Little Cadthorpe – your brain rewired itself in those few seconds. It was shocking and awful, and because of that your mind has tried to switch off from it, bury itself. But then little triggers, smells, sights, sounds, even words can make you feel like you are experiencing it again. Like it's happening again. I'm so sorry, Oliver, but I can't stop it. But you do need to believe me, it's not your fault, and it's not a sign that you are going mad. With therapy and time, you will learn to live with it and get back to a normal life, normal routines and learn how to deal with episodes when they happen.'

'You... you understand?'

'Totally.' Rory smiled at Oliver. 'Just hang in there, and know that there are people who want to help you recover, and you will. The memories, the fears even, they won't go away. But they will become manageable, and will cease to dominate your life. I promise.'

The Doctor leant forward. 'Can I borrow my friend a minute?' he said to Oliver and then led Rory aside, so they were out of earshot.

'They don't have therapists here in 1936 that can help him, Rory. I'm sorry.'

'Don't you think I know that, Doctor? I'm not stupid. But neither is he, and if I can give him just a basic security net, a basic awareness that he's not going mad, then he might start to recover a bit of his old life by himself. I'd rather he made just a five per cent improvement than leave him like this. Just knowing what is wrong helps people cope with PTSD. Them realising that others have suffered, that people understand, it makes a huge difference. And believe me, if I thought I had a way of helping him further, I'd stay here and do it.'

The Doctor smiled. 'Because that's why you became a nurse.'

'Well no, that was because I wanted to be a doctor to impress Amy, because of you, actually, Mr Raggedy Doctor. But once I started, I realised I loved it, yeah. So I can't just see him in this state of distress and ignore it.'

'You. Are. Brilliant, Rory Williams. Utterly brilliant.' The Doctor smiled. 'My mate the medic.'

Rory felt his face flush slightly at the compliment. 'And anyway, we need to find out who it is that he believes is coming back or we'll never sort out this mess.' He paused. 'At what point did we start sorting out a mess anyway? I don't remember signing up for mess-sorting-detail, when did I agree to that?'

The Doctor laughed. 'The moment we arrived Rory, the moment we arrived.'

They crossed back to where Oliver was sat in his chair, looking at a few bits of willow branch he'd broken off.

'They wore red,' he said quietly. 'Every time I see anyone in red, I flinch. And their faces...' He stared at his new friends. 'They weren't human. I knew that immediately. No one human could do what they did to those people. To my... my Daisy.' Oliver fumbled at an inside pocket of his jacket and pulled out a tattered, creased photo of the woman they'd seen in the garden. He stared straight at the Doctor. 'She didn't come back to me, did she? Earlier.'

The Doctor shook his head. 'No, Oliver, it wasn't her. I'm not sure what it was because I couldn't find her in the house.'

'You said these Weave creatures could impersonate anyone,' Rory pointed out.

The Doctor frowned. 'Yeah, and therefore it doesn't fit. Daisy – forgive me, Olly – Daisy died in Little Cadthorpe in...'

'1928,' Rory said. 'I read the reports. It was a village about thirty miles away, in Leicestershire.'

'Well, the Weave need a living, breathing person to copy. It's why they are a basically OK race – even in their rare periods of wartime they never kill their prisoners because, although their abilities make them perfect spies, they need to keep the originals alive to get a regular boost of the body pattern. And memories.'

'Daisy didn't recognise me,' Oliver muttered.

'So, not a Weave copy,' Rory said.

The Doctor shrugged. 'Oliver, when she appeared, you said other things.'

'Did I?'

'Yes, trigger words. Gas. Petroleum.'

'The things that killed Daisy, that's what they breathed. Gas. Or petrol.' He took a deep breath and shut his eyes, gripping his wheelchair. 'I can still smell it.'

Rory massaged his shoulders. 'It's OK. Deep breath. Calm down.'

The Doctor was staring upwards, into the blue sky. 'If it wasn't the Weave, then it could have been the Tahnn.'

'The who?'

'Old foes of the Weave. Neighbouring planet, nothing like the Weave, dislike for the unlike, oh look we think differently from you so you must be eradicated, and BANG you have a war. But the Tahnn can't shape change, they're just soldiers who look like prunes.'

'No!' Oliver shouted. 'No, don't let them get me.'

Rory calmed him down again.

'Ooh,' the Doctor said. 'That struck a chord. Never

been close enough to a Tahnn to smell his particular strain of halitosis but maybe we can assume that the prunefaces is what Oliver did see back in…?'

'1928.'

'Really? Now why would they go to Little Cadthorpe eight years ago, then vanish?'

Rory shrugged. 'I don't know. Perhaps they couldn't find what they wanted.'

'So why kill everyone? And yet let one man survive?' The Doctor nodded slightly towards Oliver. 'I mean, look what they did to him. We assumed it was a by-product of their attack. What if it's deliberate?'

'You think he's really a Tahnn?'

'No,' laughed the Doctor. 'But he can sniff 'em out and is convinced they're on their way back.' He paused then said: 'Rory, imagine you are an aircraft pilot. You know that Heathrow is basically in the south of England but not sure where exactly.'

'I'd be a pretty crap pilot.'

The Doctor sighed. 'Play along, please. So what are you looking for? What tells you where to land?'

'Air traffic control? Radar?'

'Imagine you have none of those, no outside radio help at all.'

'They put up airstrip lights don't they, along the runway… Oh.'

'Got there in the end. Someone's using Oliver Marks as a beacon. Eight years ago, they got the general area right but couldn't find this place. So, find one local human with a war-damaged mind already, someone susceptible to their form of shock tactics and send him out into the world. Eventually, if you are patient enough, someone sees that beacon and brings him to what you are looking for.'

Rory nodded excitedly. 'And once they found this burial mound here and thought it was the Weave ship, they brought Oliver here to act as a homing beacon to the rest of the Tahnn.'

'Except no one here is a Tahnn, or our sniffer dog there would've spotted them.'

'The first Mrs Porter,' suggested Rory. 'She brought him to Shalford Heights, but now she's dead or whatever. Perhaps she was the disguised Tahnn.'

'Could be. We need to get access to the Weave ship.'

'Which is buried inside that mound under the school that Enola Porter is going to open any day now?'

'That lived in the house that Jack built. Spot on, Rory.' The Doctor spoke to Oliver. 'I need to meet Enola Porter. How do I do that?'

Oliver shrugged. 'Just go to the dig, she never leaves it these days except to sleep. And sometimes she stays at the school to do that with the rest of her team.'

'Does she? Doesn't come home much. Interesting.'

'Is it?'

'Actually not a lot. Although it suggests she isn't as close to her husband as he likes to make out. After all, it's only a ten-minute walk home.'

'Tell her you're aliens,' Oliver said suddenly. 'That'll pique her interest enough to give you the time of day.'

'I'm not an alien,' said Rory.

Oliver shrugged. 'Might as well be. You're not like those ones that killed Daisy, but there's still something strange about you two.'

'Pot meet a black kettle,' murmured the Doctor. 'Look, I don't know what's going to happen next, Oliver, but I do know this. I need you. I need you now like no one has ever needed you before. Do you trust me?'

'Yes.' Oliver didn't hesitate for once. Rory's compassion and concern had earned them both that.

'Good man.' The Doctor smiled at him and winked. 'Shall we go save planet Earth?'

'Or die trying.' Oliver nodded. 'Absolutely.'

'Not so keen on the dying bit, to be really honest,' the Doctor said. 'But whatever floats your boat.'

Chapter
8

Enola Porter stood proudly in front of the small marquee erected in the school playground. She was pouring a cup of tea from a steel teapot, and then passing it to one of her fellow archaeologists. After doing this for a while, she began unwrapping cakes.

But she was no meek society woman by the look of it. She was dressed in a white shirt stained with sweat, a canvas over-jacket and a small peaked cap, with a pair of plus-fours which were tucked into knee-high black woollen socks, and heavy hobnailed boots. The only dash of colour was what looked like an old school tie (red and blue stripes) in place of a belt, although it was most likely more for decoration than for keeping her plus-fours up.

'Blimey,' the Doctor said quietly to Rory as they

entered the school grounds, pushing Oliver along in his chair. 'Enola Porter's a man.'

Rory did a double-take. 'Really?'

The Doctor sighed. 'Of course not. I just meant in a Lady Gaga meets George Kirrin kind of way.'

'Who?'

'Lady Gaga?'

'No, I know Lady Gaga. Well, not "know" know, but I know who she is,' Rory explained. 'But not who – hang on. Lady Gaga's not a man!'

'Well, obviously,' the Doctor said. 'But when she first started out, they all said she was. Course, give it a few more years, when the real truth is revealed, and then watch the furore kick off. One of those gossipy magazines pay her "entourage",' the Doctor mimed the quote marks, 'their biggest ever payout to get the truth behind which dimensional rift she really fell through. Oh yes!' The Doctor stopped. 'Hang on. Do I mean Lady Gaga or the other one?'

'Which other one?'

'Won *The X Factor*. Or *American Idol*. Or was it *South Korea's Got Talent*? Either way, Enola Porter is a bit butch.'

'Charming,' Rory murmured, as Enola strode manfully towards them. 'OK,' he said even more quietly. 'You may have a point.'

She stuck out a dusty, scarred and deeply tanned hand which Rory shook.

Yup, he'd had patients after a Saturday night fight in Gloucester with pussier handshakes than that.

Fearful for the continued operation of his fingers, he eased his hand out, and Enola Porter shook hands with the Doctor, who didn't flinch at all, of course.

'My name's the Doctor. This is Rory. And of course you know our chum Olly.'

Enola kissed Oliver's cheek. 'You must think this is important, Oliver, to trek all the way down here.'

'These people believe me, Enola!'

Enola looked at each of them in turn. 'Really?' she said after a moment. 'I see.'

The Doctor smiled his smiliest smile.

'Well, Doctor, a real pleasure to meet you.'

'I gather you're quite the archaeologist,' he said.

Enola Porter laughed lightly. 'You sound like my husband, but without the actual patronising tone. Maybe you hide it better.'

'Not at all. I am genuinely interested in your work.'

'Of course,' Enola said, probably unconvinced. 'This is an amazing find.' She nudged a rucksack beside a table with her foot. 'All in my notebooks, all my travels, all my discoveries. I shall need a whole new book once this dig is completed.'

'I should like to read them,' the Doctor said. 'I imagine you have had a most interesting life.'

'Thank you. I have. Oh, and I must introduce you to my team – be darned rude not to, yes? Now then, who first?' She looked around the schoolyard at the various people pouring tea, moving shovels, or chatting. Most of them, Rory guessed, were the few locals still in the village, but a few stood out as academics or, at least, were clearly not locals. They didn't have that 'village' look about them.

'Well, over there, that's Christopher Maginn, always fascinated by rocks we find. Crystal, diamonds, things like that.'

A thin man in his forties, wearing a dark suit that really should have been at an awards ceremony not a dig, waved from behind a cup of tea.

'And over there with the ridiculous moustache, that's young Hamish Ridley. He's another geologist but is very into fossils and dinosaurs. And a teller of tall tales, so watch out for that. Says he helped Howard Carter excavate Tutankhamun's tomb, but as he's not died of the curse yet, not sure we believe him, what.' Enola laughed gaily.

She pointed next to a sour-faced old man who, Rory suspected, had not eaten for about thirty years. His skin was taut over his frame to such an extent that Rory wondered if he could actually see the individual bones in his face and hands.

'Good afternoon, Marten,' Enola bellowed, but he ignored her. She grinned at the Doctor, Rory and Oliver. 'Oh I know I shouldn't tease but he's so wretched and miserable, and it's all an act. Got kicked out of the Bauhaus in '32, probably too much of a Nazi for them, but a brilliant draughtsman. Draws everything we find around the world. Not as fast as a photographer, but so much more accurate. He gets depth and scale and emotional context and

– oh look, see that chap there, with the monocle? That's Walpole Spune, he's our local expert on stone circles, burial mounds, dolomites and so forth. Only been with the team a couple of months. It was he who found evidence that the dig was more than just a burial ground.'

'Interesting,' said Rory. 'How local is local?'

'Oh, a couple of counties across. Comes from somewhere near Lincoln, I think.'

'And he told you to dig here?'

'He was instrumental in getting us started, yes.'

Finally able to get a word in, the Doctor asked if it wasn't *just* a burial ground, what was it?

'Oh, come see,' said Enola, taking the cup of tea out of Maginn's hand as they walked past, draining it and returning it all in one swift movement. She also chose to ignore the look of daggers that Maginn gave in return, so Rory shrugged an apology, but Maginn ignored him.

Enola patted Oliver's shoulder. 'Can't take your chair down with us, Mr Marks, sorry. Will you be OK up here? Shall I get one of my stout volunteers to pop you home?'

Oliver shook his head. 'I don't need the blasted chair. I can walk, you know.'

'Yes, we know,' said Rory patiently. 'But you've been medicated quite heavily, and I would be happier if I knew you were safe up here, not having a stumble or something in the dark, yeah?'

Oliver looked at Rory, and his shoulders seemed

to sag. Then he smiled weakly at Enola. 'I'd rather wait here for the Doctor and Rory until they're finished.'

Enola nodded her understanding and asked one of the ladies to nip over.

It was Nancy Thirman from the library. Rory was about to say something, but the Doctor gave a tiny shake of the head, so he let it go.

'Nan will look after you,' said Enola to Oliver.

'Of course I will,' Nancy Thirman said sweetly.

Rory got closer to the Doctor. 'She's—'

'Your ball of living wool?'

'How did you know?'

'Your face said it. Frankly, you could've had a pink neon sign saying, "Doctor, it's an alien" hovering above your head, although that might have been too subtle.'

'Is it safe to leave Oliver with her?'

'He hasn't reacted to her Weave-ness, so I think so, yes. Means it's definitely the Tahnn he's wired up to spot. Which makes me think… nah, never mind. Let's follow the lady.'

So they followed Enola out of the school playground and over to a huge tented area covering most of the rugby field at the back. The goalposts had been dismantled and were lying together at the side of the pitch, but everything else was hidden by the canvas.

Enola yanked back a flap at one end and bade them follow her in, so they did.

In front of them, illuminated by flickering temporary electrical torches hung with string, was a path leading to a hole in the ground. Looking down, they saw that it led to a gaping maw beneath the field.

Enola scooped up a massive torch and switched it on, casting strange shadows across the canvas behind them. So strange that for a second Rory thought he had two shadows until he realised that the German artist, Marten, was stood behind him, sketchpad and pencil ready, looking like a schoolchild on an excursion to a brass-rubbing centre. (Rory had been on those when at school. He hated them. But they'd stayed in his memory.) Of course, Marten's less than hospitable face reminded Rory more of a teacher than a pupil. A sickly, pale teacher who was either going to bite your head off or keel over and die in the next ten minutes; either could happen. Rory had known teachers like that, too. Usually they were the ones who thought brass rubbing was exciting, informative and creative.

If the Doctor even noticed Marten had joined them, he certainly didn't react to his presence. Instead he was looking around the tunnelled entrance that seemed to be taking them further and further below the rugby field.

'I'm impressed.' He whistled through his teeth, which confirmed to Rory that he was, indeed, impressed. Often the Doctor would say 'I'm impressed' when he wasn't impressed at all (frequently when it was something Rory had done, and the 'I'm impressed' was followed by a wink between the Doctor and Amy that they believed Rory hadn't seen). That was an insincere 'I'm impressed'. This was a sincere one.

Hmmm. He needed to talk to Amy about that winking thing.

'I'm also confused,' the Doctor added.

That was a new one on Rory.

'I mean,' he continued, 'this is a dig. Quite literally. But you talked about a burial mound. This is more of a burial pit, really.'

'We call them graves,' Rory found himself adding with a laugh and then wishing he hadn't.

'No, not a grave, Rory,' the Doctor said, quite seriously. 'Although I can see the analogy. But look ahead. That's definitely a mound. It's just way underground.'

'I know,' said Enola Porter. 'How unique is that?'

'Well, dunno about unique,' the Doctor countered cheerfully, 'but definitely on the unusual side. Wouldn't you agree, Marten?' he called back, acknowledging the grumpy German for the first time.

'Ja,' Marten said. Or grunted. Rory wasn't sure so he gave him the benefit of the doubt. He glanced back and saw that Marten was sketching like mad.

The Doctor's attention was now on the actual mound itself because, sure enough, there it was.

A huge long peapod-shaped colossus beneath the earth.

'How did you know it was here?' the Doctor asked. 'It's not like you've invented infrared scanners or seismographic radar yet.'

Enola stared at the Doctor, a frown on her face for the first time. 'I have no idea what those things are,' she said.

'Good for you,' the Doctor beamed. 'Cos if you had, well, Rory would have been worried, wouldn't you, Rory?'

'Why would Rory have been worried?' Enola asked.

'Because they've not been invented yet,' Rory said, 'and that would imply some kind of alien or temporal anomaly or interference of the kind the Doctor doesn't like.'

The Doctor slapped Rory on the back. 'Spot on. Bit too much information, to be honest, matey,' he added, 'but my fault for thinking you'd know when not to show off.' He turned to Enola. 'But he's right. Rory's from 2010, when these things are commonplace. Me, ooooh, a lot further away. So now we've waved our intergalactic credentials at you and no doubt blown away your mind with our brilliance, sophistication and sexy alien hair – that's just me by the way, Rory's hair is neither alien nor sexy – why don't you answer my question? How did you know a burial mound was buried under a school rugger pitch in 1936?'

'Easy,' Enola said. 'Walpole Spune got his divining rod out and led us straight to it.'

'A divining rod?' asked Rory. 'Really?'

The Doctor nodded. 'I so want one of those, Rory. A bit of old twig that leads you to things. So simple. Who needs a TARDIS or a sonic screwdriver when a bit of tree branch will do?'

'No one,' Rory said. 'It's nonsense.'

'Ah,' the Doctor countered. 'You know that. I know that. But Walpole Spune doesn't; he believes. And faith in your own abilities is both useful and powerful.'

'Are you saying he really did divine his way to this place?' Rory was gobsmacked.

'Naaah,' the Doctor said. 'But this lot of primitives do. Sorry, no offence,' he threw to Enola. 'And that means someone has let them believe it because they wanted to be found. Now then, where's Marten got to?'

Sure enough, the German had vanished, presumably back the way they'd come. Rory walked over to where he'd been sketching and found a sheet of foolscap drawing paper. He looked at the image. And sighed.

'Doctor,' he called. 'You need to see this.'

The Doctor was at his side in an instant. 'What's up?'

Rory showed him the drawing Marten had done, and the Doctor blew air out of his cheeks.

'Curiouser and curiouser,' he said and turned

back to Enola. 'Does Marten often draw things like this?'

She joined them and started as she looked at the sketch and said, quite definitively, that she'd never seen anything like it before. At first glance, it looked like a charcoal sketch of the Doctor and Rory in the tunnels with Enola Porter. Except that instead of where their heads and faces would normally have been, the Doctor and Rory appeared to have been drawn with balls of dark wool instead.

'Baaaa,' the Doctor said. 'I had wondered what my four-legged chum was trying to tell me this morning.'

Rory tapped the paper. 'Something else weird,' he said.

The Doctor looked at it and frowned. 'Nope, not seeing your problem.'

Rory sighed and started counting backwards from twenty.

Shooting him an annoyed look, the Doctor stared harder. As Rory went from 4 to 3, the Doctor snapped, 'All right, I got it at 18. I was just trying to work out how he did that.'

Enola shrugged. 'I don't see what else is unusual other than your heads being woolly,' she said.

The Doctor smiled at her. 'Describe Rory. Real Rory, not charcoal Rory.'

Enola looked at him. 'Tall, fair-haired, not stunningly good-looking but not ugly either…'

'Thanks for that.' Rory snatched the paper away

and all but shoved it in her face. 'He hasn't drawn what I'm wearing today.'

Enola shrugged. 'He's imaginative. It's that kind of creativity—'

'What Rory means,' said the Doctor gently, 'is that your friend Marten has drawn me in an old brown suit I've not… fitted into for a while and Rory in his work clothes. That's what a nurse wears where he comes from.'

If Enola was thrown by this, she was more thrown by the knowledge Rory was a nurse. 'You? A nurse? A woman's job?'

'Equality works both ways in the future,' Rory countered. 'I like the way a male nurse throws you, but you accepted the Doctor is an alien and I'm from seventy or eighty years away without missing a beat.'

Enola shrugged. 'I've seen a lot of strange things on my travels, sir. If I hadn't opened my mind up to accept that there is more in this universe than the Good Book and learned preachers tell us, I'd be pretty poor at what I do.'

'Have you met aliens before?' asked the Doctor gently.

'Not that I am aware of, Doctor. But I don't rule out that possibility, of course not. I'd be foolish to do so.'

'Aliens, OK. But time travel. That's usually a harder sell.'

Enola didn't reply at first, and then she nodded at

Rory. '2010, you said. Well, that explains why I can't understand half of what you two have been going on about. The future.' She turned to the Doctor. 'Am I famous?'

'Sorry?'

'In archaeology circles?'

The Doctor smiled. 'Are you kidding? Blimey, I've waited years to meet you. Harry Balfour, Howard Carter, Marcus Scarman, Shinichi Fujimura, Indiana Jones, Gordon Childe, Benny Summerfield, Constantine Gedes and Enola Porter. The greats. The true greats.' The Doctor winked at her and pointed back to the burial mound. 'And you know what puts you up there with them? That does, Mrs Porter. Because as you are going to discover very shortly, what's under there is no Bronze Age chieftain, no medieval king, or whatever else you expect to find in a fogou like this. Inside there is an honest-to-goodness alien starship, and you find it, Mrs Porter. You and your team live in history for the first evidence brought before the public about the existence of aliens.' He hugged her tightly. 'Cor, I love you, Mrs Enola Porter. That's why I'm here. Me and Rory. And Amy Pond. We wanted to meet you before you became too famous to get near.'

'Me?'

'Yup. We're on a sort of Time Team, y'see. Future people can swing back in time and discover real archaeology at work. And now we need to go, leave you to get on with it. Or you know, the time continuum goes *poof!* and we never exist or kill our grandfathers or go home and find everyone we loved looks like a butterfly. Bye then. Good luck.'

'Bye,' Rory added lamely, giving a little wave as the Doctor almost hauled him out of the tunnels and back out through the marquee.

When they reached the school building and he was sure they were alone, Rory stopped moving. After a second or two, the Doctor noticed and wandered back to him.

'What?'

Rory shook his head. 'How many of your wretched laws of time did you just break? I mean, so it's not OK for me and Amy to do it, but it's OK for you?'

'Nope, that's not true.'

'It's not?'

'Nope, Amy can break 'em too. Only you can't. Because you have a gob on you, and you never know when enough is enough.'

'Oh.'

The Doctor punched Rory's arm in a playful way that suggested he'd not actually tried it before, which was confirmed by Rory's 'ouch'.

'Another thing not to do again,' Rory told him.

The Doctor pouted. 'Aw. Quite liked doing that.' He smiled. 'I was joking, by the way, Rory. You're getting the hang of this time-travelling lark.'

'Even if I am,' Rory replied, 'I'm still confused. I'm not an archaeologist, but I've heard of Howard

Carter. And Indiana Jones,' he said pointedly. 'But how come I've never heard of Enola Porter? If she has discovered aliens, I think that might have permeated through the History curriculum by the time I went to school.'

The Doctor nodded. 'My thoughts exactly. Even I haven't heard of her, and I've heard of everyone,' he said.

'Heard of who?' asked Amy, suddenly standing behind Rory.

'You have to stop doing that,' Rory said, touching his chest. 'One day I'll have a coronary, and it'll be your fault.'

'Ooh, sorrrrry,' she said and kissed his neck. 'So, who haven't you heard of, Doctor?'

'Enola Porter,' he said. 'She's—'

'The archaeologist?' Amy laughed. 'Wow. I mean, wow! Rory, we're finally ahead of the Doctor.'

Rory frowned. 'You what?'

Amy shrugged. 'She's mega-famous, Doctor. Discovered evidence of aliens in some Roman-y Iron Age-y burial mound, yeah? Did her in Year Ten.'

The Doctor looked at Amy for a second, then laughed. 'Course you did. Rory must have been in the remedial class.' He gave Rory a look that both challenged him to argue and simultaneously suggested, for his own continued health, it'd be best not to.

Or at least that was how Rory interpreted it.

The Doctor threw his arms around their

shoulders. 'Let's find Oliver Marks and head back to the Manse for some grub. I'm famished. Besides which...' He hauled Enola Porter's canvas bag of notebooks off the ground. 'I have some reading to catch up on.'

'Isn't that theft?' asked Rory.

'Not if he gets them back before she notices,' said Amy.

'Your young girl's got a point,' said the Doctor, and Rory almost winced as he anticipated the tirade from Amy at the 'your girl' quip.

But Amy shrugged. 'Food sounds good,' she said. 'Omm nom nom.' She led the way back.

Chapter
9

Amy Pond was a pretty certain kind of person. She was pretty certain it had been Shirley Morgan who had nicked the sweets from the Leadworth Post Office when she was 10. She was pretty certain that Darren Cotham had knowingly lied when he'd told her that Pernod was all aniseed and no alcohol when she was 13. She was pretty certain that Doctor Griffiths had had more on his mind than psychological counselling when she was 14. She was pretty sure that biting him had been a good move, too. And, of course, she'd been pretty certain that her Raggedy Doctor existed.

So she was pretty sure, on all the available evidence, that she was in a whole host of trouble right now.

It was the fault of the wretched tree made of wool, she decided (and there was a phrase she'd never expected to think in her life). One minute she'd been touching it, feeling its weird movement beneath her fingers, the next it had reached up and grabbed her like a bad outtake from the *Lord of the Rings* movies and pulled her into... into what? The bark? The wool? The centre of the Earth?

If this was the centre of Earth, shouldn't it be hot? Or full of bad stop-motion dinosaurs and Doug McClure in a torn shirt and bad Seventies hair? (She'd won her team a lot of kudos in a pub quiz once for knowing his name – oh yes, she knew her bad movies.) And, above all, shouldn't it be dark?

There was a dull green glow, which immediately reminded her of the yellowy-green of the woolly tree. So there had to be a connection (hooray for time spent with the Doctor teaching her that).

Amy tried to move, to get up from wherever it was the tree had dumped her, but her left ankle was held down by a tree root. She didn't bother finding out if that was made of wool, too – she just chose to assume it was. Besides which, it had a degree of give in it and didn't seem to be digging into her skin, so yeah, woolly stumpy thingy was holding her where she was.

'Hullo?' she called out. 'My name is Amy Pond, and I'm really very nice and not at all a danger to you. Whoever you are. Woolly tree things. Or whatever.'

No reply.

Quelle surprise.

The greeny-yellowy glow was good, and her eyes were adjusting with each passing second, so before long she could make out that she was in a circular chamber with a long corridor leading out of it. That itself faded into complete darkness, so she had no idea how long it was, but 'quite' seemed a good guess.

Tom Benson. Where the hell was Tom Benson?

He'd got her here, under false pretences of being nice, kind, slightly jealous of Rory and what was it? Oh yeah. Human. Pretending to be human.

'Oi, Tom Benson, where are you?' she bellowed as loud as she could.

There was no response, but she saw a shape in the darkness ahead. It didn't move as much as… well, OK, it did move. But it moved in a strange way Amy couldn't put her finger on. It sort of floated. No – floated wasn't right. Flowed. Wafted. Like it wasn't quite solid. And yet she saw it.

'Not helping yourself, Pond,' she muttered aloud, hoping that might draw it out again.

And then she realised it was in the area between the corridor and the chamber she was held in. One second, space, the next, a… thing.

'Don't come any closer,' she said, then paused. 'Unless you are here to rescue me, in which case come as close as you like.'

The 'thing' dropped to the floor, and Amy realised

it was like a soft ball of something. Oh, of course. It was a ball of wool. Earth had been invaded by the associates of the local Women's Institute.

The ball quivered for a second and then started to grow, reshaping itself. As she watched in horrified fascination, it shaped and smoothed and eased itself into a woollen copy of a human figure. It reminded Amy of those little wooden blank figures that artists used to draw human shapes with.

After a few seconds, she was faced by a greeny-yellowy woman, with a face that seemed to be knitted, but with definite eyes, mouth, nose all formed by the wool (or whatever it was) just being slightly differently shaped or indented.

Amy couldn't stop herself. 'Wow,' she said. 'Wow, that's astonishing.'

'Thank you, Amy,' said the woollen woman. 'Apologies for scaring you. The person you know as Tom Benson was meant to bring you here voluntarily, not through the... tree?'

Amy nodded, like this was the most casual conversation in the world. 'Yeah, tree,' she confirmed. 'Nice tree. Must've taken ages to knit those.'

The woollen woman laughed. 'Seconds. The Weave can manipulate ourselves into any shape for short periods, but what you see now is our basic shape.'

'The Weave? You?'

The woman nodded. 'I am 128. The Commander of the WSS *Exalted*. We crashed here centuries ago.'

'Wow,' Amy said again. 'And you've not conquered us, or enslaved us or wiped us out yet? Cool.'

128 shrugged. 'We wish the people of this planet no harm. We are no threat, we are just trying to survive.'

'Underground?'

'That's safest for now. We realised when we awoke that this era wasn't ready for us. They had not encountered enough other species to accept us for what we are.'

'But you're telling me.'

128 laughed. 'You are not from this planet. Like us.'

'I most certainly am,' Amy said.

A frown wove across 128's forehead and then vanished again. It was fascinating, Amy realised, the way 128's movements were fluid, how nothing she did was ever still.

'If you are from Earth, you are unique amongst these humans.'

Amy shrugged. 'Aye, that's us. Unique, amazing and the bestest.'

128 blinked slowly, digesting this information. 'We assumed you, the Doctor and Rory Williams were travellers like us. You arrived in a capsule – 456195 saw you!'

'45... what?'

'You call him Tom Benson.'

'This is 1936,' Amy explained. 'Right?'

The Commander nodded. 'So I understand.'

'I'm from 2010.'

128 blinked slowly.

'The future.'

128 blinked again and tilted her head, thinking.

'Me. And Rory. 2010. June to be precise. Getting married, too. If we make it back.' She raised her left hand. 'Look. Engagement ring. Cost a fortune, so of course Rory doesn't like me wearing it too often. He thinks I'll lose it. As if.'

'Time travel. On this planet?'

'The Doctor. From a place called Mars. Sounds chocolatey to me, but apparently it's like "woooooh, long way away". His ship brought us here.'

128 raised her hand. Amy watched in amazement as something grew out of it and separated itself, like a woolly smartphone. 128 tapped at it and frowned. Then the frown just melted away again. So did the smartphone thing.

'The name "Mars" means nothing to our computers, but the Weave don't know everything – every race has different names for the planets of the universe. And the galaxies may have changed a great deal during our time trapped down here. Planets come and go.'

'It's a big red planet, up there.' Amy pointed straight up. 'On a clear night you can see it.'

'Planet S4,' said 128. 'I know the one you mean.'

Amy opted to change the subject. 'How long have you been here?'

'Six thousand years, give or take,' 128 said. 'But we awoke only fifteen years ago. Our systems malfunctioned after the crash. We were supposed to be woken within hours of arrival, but the trigger mechanism was damaged. We awoke only when our secondary systems overrode it because of the presence of the Tahnn.'

'The who?'

'The Tahnn. We were under attack by them. They have been hunting our people for millennia. It would appear that they haven't given up, though centuries have passed. They must have finally worked out where we were and sent a raiding party to find us. They failed, but their presence was enough to trigger our alarms and wake us.'

As Amy let this all sink in, a horrible thought crossed her mind. 'You're the leader of these Weave people?'

128 nodded.

'And you've just told me, a total stranger, everything about your mission.'

'I've told you very little, actually, but enough for you to understand. And enough for us to get a basic grasp of who you are, how you think, what you say.'

'You're going to kill me, aren't you?'

128 laughed. 'No, don't be silly. But we can't let you go. Not yet. Though I promise we will.'

'When?'

'Once we are safe from the Tahnn.'

Amy thought about this. 'Umm, excuse me but if these Tahnn have been chasing you for a few centuries and not found you, then you might be around here for, oh, let's say, longer than a week or two?'

128 shrugged. 'We wait for millennia if need be. I will not risk exposure to the Tahnn. That's why we have infiltrated this settlement, I have placed my own people in there, partly to supply the rest of us with food and drink but also to keep the *Exalted* safe from prying eyes.'

Amy nodded. 'You know there's a huge dig up top, trying to unearth you?'

128 nodded. 'We will deal with that when necessary.'

'Deal with it how, exactly?'

128 smiled and for the first time Amy felt uncomfortable with the Commander. Because it wasn't a particularly nice smile.

'In whatever way I deem necessary to protect my people, Amy. But it's all right. It's why I had you brought here. You are going to help me.'

'I am? Really? Are you sure.'

128's smartphone thingie grew from her hand again, and she thumbed something on it.

'Instant app for dealing with irritating archaeologists?' quipped Amy, trying to sound less concerned than she was.

In answer, the wall to her right bulged, and another figure stepped out of what Amy now realised was not earth but the same wool texture as 128.

'Hullo,' she said. 'I'm the ship's counsellor. 6011. Pleased to meet you, Amy Pond.'

'Back atcha.' Amy said quietly. 'Don't get too close. I bite counsellors.'

6011 ignored this. She suddenly shivered and started changing shape and colour. It was like watching a sweater or socks being knitted in front of her, but on fast forward. Except this wasn't just clothing, Amy realised; it was a person.

Less than a minute later, Amy faced a duplicate Amy Pond, every detail perfect.

'Is my bum really that small? Wow, I look hot,' Amy said. 'When Rory and I have our first post-wedding dance, I'm going to look fantastic. Thank you for the compliment.'

128 shrugged. 'I'm glad you accept what we're doing, Amy. Thank you.'

'Like I have a choice,' Amy replied, pointing at the root holding her firmly in place. 'So what happens to me while Counsellor Copycat here is running around up there trying to be me?'

'Same as the real Tom Benson, and the others. Sleep.'

'Not tired, actually,' Amy said.

Another of the Weave grew into solidity by the doorway. 'I am 107863,' he said, 'and this won't hurt a bit.'

'I've heard that before. It's never true.'

The last thing Amy saw was a long green tendril of wool shoot from 107863's hand to the woollen root holding Amy's ankle. She felt a slight jolt go through her body and she slumped to the soft ground, which felt more like a comfortable woollen carpet than she thought it should. Her head was spinning, but she could still hear the voices of the Weave.

'She'll be out in seconds, Commander.' That was the newcomer. 'The anaesthetic has passed through her skin.'

'Thank you, Medic 107863,' said 128. 'Let's hope only a few years pass before we need to wake her again.'

Years?

Amy had to hope the Doctor got the warning. Or Rory.

Rory.

'I love you, Rory,' she managed to mutter.

Then blackness swirled into her mind and she was unconscious.

Chapter
10

'You are beautiful, sexy and really hot. Woof!' The Doctor
gave Rory a wink. 'You're not bad either, Rory.'

Rory just shuffled awkwardly and hoped no one
took the Doctor seriously. 'This is 1936,' he reminded
the Doctor.

The Doctor shrugged. He was facing a group of
staff at the Manse, but had actually been directly
addressing a magnificent Aga that took pride of
place in the kitchen where they were gathered. He
had a hand on one of two oven doors and the other
hand on a pot of boiling potatoes on the hob.

The cook, Mrs Stern, blushed at the attention her
kitchen was getting. 'Oh, sir, you are too kind,' she
said shyly.

It wasn't a big staff, Rory noted. A cook, two

young maids, that manservant and quiet Old John sat in a corner cleaning spoons with a cloth. In fact, he seemed to be cleaning the same spoon. Over and over again.

'We were just with Mrs Porter at the dig, and she told us to come and seek you out, Mrs Stock—'

'Stern,' Rory hissed.

'Thought I was being quite polite actually,' the Doctor responded less subtly. He returned to the task at hand. 'Anyway, so your Mrs Porter, she says to my main man Rory here, and lovely Amy who has gone to powder her nose or something, that we needed to taste some of your excellent culinary skills, Mrs Stick. So while she's busy at the dig, we thought we'd come see if we can get some grub before we head back and carry on digging with her team.'

'I'll bring you some of my finest pheasant up to the dining room shortly, Doctor,' she said smiling the sort of big rosy smile that Rory associated with big fat cooks from storybooks.

'No no, no,' the Doctor sat on a wooden chair by the rough kitchen table, scarred with years of chopping vegetables and charred by hot pots. He pointed at the table. 'None of that fancy stuff for us, Mrs S. I'd rather spend some time chatting to you lovely people.'

The manservant who Rory thought might have been called Chibbers or Chiggers sighed loudly and shooed away the maids. 'No time for you girls to sit listening to the chit-chat of your betters,' he said. 'There's a Manse to clean up.'

The two girls bobbed politely to 'them London types' (as Rory had heard Chibbers/Chiggers refer to them when he thought he couldn't be heard earlier) and nipped away, giggling quietly.

'That's enough,' Chibbers/Chiggers snapped as he followed them out.

'So, Mrs S,' the Doctor said cheerfully, 'how many years you been in service?'

'Since I was 14, sir. Started off as a kitchen maid to the Southwolds, then I trained as a cook at one of the big London hotels before working in a few homes here in the East. Been with the Porters seven years now.'

'And Mr Stern?' Rory asked.

'Ooh, never time for any of that, sir,' Mrs Stern said with a smile as she stirred some vegetables.

'The "Mrs" is an honorific, Rory. Always is in the big houses for a cook. Gives 'em a sense of place and position.' The Doctor smiled back at Mrs Stern. 'So... you must've known the first Mrs Porter.'

Rory could sense the atmosphere change, like someone had flicked a switch.

'I did indeed,' was Mrs Stern's only response and, unseen by her, the Doctor gave Rory an 'ooh, get her' look.

'Sooooo...' He tried changing the subject. 'Cooking been a lifelong hobby...'

Mrs Stern's expression darkened a little.

'No, not just a hobby,' said the Doctor quickly. 'A passion! A passion that's also your job! How... er...' He found himself flailing and looked hopefully at Mrs Stern.

'I enjoy it, sir,' was her curt but-trying-to-be-polite reply.

Rory suspected they had outstayed their welcome. 'Doctor, why don't we leave Mrs Stern to her kitchen while we join Amy and freshen up for dinner?'

The Doctor responded with an 'oh do shut up' look.

Old John suddenly stopped cleaning his spoon, stood up and walked over to them, his limp more pronounced than ever. Rory guessed he was in his sixties, so it was most likely a war wound from the Boer.

'I have to check on Mr Marks,' Old John said to Mrs Stern, but he gave Rory and the Doctor a swift nod of the head as he passed them. This seemed to mean 'follow me and learn things to your advantage' and not 'I have a really embarrassing spasm in my neck', so they followed him out.

'We'll eat in the dining room, after all,' the Doctor called to Mrs Stern, but she didn't reply.

'You've upset the old woman,' Old John said as they walked down one of the long gloomy corridors. 'Not difficult.'

'She seemed such a nice cheerful lady, though,' moaned the Doctor.

'Oh, that's the professional bit. Deep down, she's like everyone else in this village. Weird.'

'And you're not,' said Rory, hoping that sounded less rude to Old John than it did in his head.

'No, I'm normal. Me and Mr Marks. The only ones that are. Your fault, though, you asked about Mrs Porter. The real one.'

'Real one?' said Rory, abruptly aware that staring at Old John's limping leg probably wasn't helping.

'That's what they call her. They don't like the new one. I reckon it's cos nobody got invited to the wedding.'

'I'm missing something,' the Doctor said quietly.

Rory frowned. 'What?'

'Amy Pond. Where's she got to? One minute she's all omm nom nom, next thing she wants to explore the place. You need to keep a closer eye on your soon-to-be-wife, Rory.'

'I do?'

'I think so. Still, she'll be along presently. In fact…'

He held up his hand and slowly lowered each finger individually, counting them off soundlessly.

One. Two. Three. Four. Five.

As his thumb went down, Rory's heart jumped a bit as his fiancée's voice rang out. 'Oh, there you are,' Amy said from the far end of the corridor.

'Had fun exploring, Pond?' the Doctor asked. 'This gentleman's filling us in on all the weird goings-on here.'

'I am?' said Old John.

'He is?' said Amy. 'I see.'

The Doctor turned to the older man. 'Tell you what, you go and see to Olly, and leave us here. We'll make our way to the dining room and wait for our pleasant pheasant to arrive.'

'Pleasant pheasant,' said Amy. 'Mmmm, love it.'

Rory frowned at this, wondering when Amy had ever eaten pheasant. Mind you, she'd seen and done so many things with the Doctor that anything was possible.

Yet something didn't seem right.

'Tom Benson showed me the whole village,' she said. 'Seems very peaceful.'

'Really?' said the Doctor. 'That's nice.'

'Well, Earth's always my favourite planet,' joked Rory, thinking about the Doctor's comment earlier, when they had first arrived.

'Yes, all right, I like it too,' he said. 'Home from home.'

'One day you should take us to your home,' Amy said. 'I've always wanted to go there.'

The Doctor said nothing, just frowned a bit. 'Why?' he said after a moment.

'Mars is always such a beautiful sight. On some nights, you can see it glowing in the night sky. All red and orange.'

The Doctor shrugged. 'Yes, it is rather beautiful.' He pointed forward. 'But for now, I just want some lunch.'

Amy nodded and took Rory's hand in hers.

'Come on, sexy fiancé,' she said. 'Escort me to the table like a true gentlemen.'

Rory smiled back at her. 'This way, madam.'

Chapter
11

If the people of 1936 had possessed telescopes like those used by the people of Rory's era, they might have spotted the Tahnn ship.

It was in space, hovering somewhere between Io and Callisto, shielded from the sunlight (such as it was) by the gas giant known as Jupiter.

These names would have meant nothing to the Tahnn. Not only did they not have names for alien moons or planets, they had no interest in them either. All that mattered to the Tahnn was fulfilling their mission: find the Weave ship, access it, then totally destroy it and its occupants.

It was a mission that had lasted for thousands of years. But they had a means to complete it now. As soon as the ship had been uncovered, they would be able to home in on it, get what they wanted and then vaporise it completely. It was unfortunate for their agent on the planet concerned that he too would be destroyed in the localised conflagration, but Tahnnis Command had made the decision not to pre-warn him of this. It was neater that way.

Some years back, a troop had installed a beacon on the planet in the usual way. They had then vaporised themselves, bar one who would act as guardian to the beacon and activate it once the Weave ship was located.

Of course, they could just destroy the entire planet, which would be quicker and easier and ensure that there were no survivors, but that would bring down the wrath of the Shadow Proclamation. As powerful as the Tahnn were, they knew their limits and how… determined the Shadow Architect could be. They'd encountered witnesses and heard stories of forces from another galaxy that had crossed into this one and infringed on the Shadow Proclamation's territory. They had wiped out an entire species over a dispute no one could recall.

The Shadow Proclamation had, under the cover of diplomacy, crossed the boundaries of space and reached that far galaxy, seeding it with a virus. Guilty or innocent, if any of the inhabitants of any of that galaxy's worlds ever tried leaving their planetary atmosphere, the virus would be triggered. It would wipe out the entire galaxy in a matter of hours.

Of course, one planet had risen to the challenge

and to the stars. One planet was dead in minutes. The other worlds pleaded with the Shadow Proclamation for aid – it had not been their fault. But the Shadow Proclamation couldn't – or wouldn't – help that quickly, and over one-third of the galaxy died in agony that day. By the time the antidote was provided, a lesson had been learned: threaten the Shadow Proclamation, its articles or covenants, its worlds or territories, and retribution would be swift and devastating.

It was entirely possible this story was a complete fabrication but, as a piece of propaganda, it was effective. The Tahnn could get away with destroying one area of the Weave's hiding place. Probably. But to destroy a whole non-combatant world just to get at the Weave treasure... well, it wasn't worth the risk.

And so the plan had been hatched: get in, locate the Weave, destroy them, cauterise the immediate locality if unavoidable, then get out before anyone could raise the alarm. The dominant indigenous species on the planet concerned was of a low status, and they were unlikely to be aware of the existence of the Shadow Proclamation, let alone have the means to contact them.

Which was all well and good until their periodic scans and communiqués with their agent there reported the arrival of an alien with two hearts, an IQ well beyond the normal range of the planet's inhabitants and a strange blue box that defied both

Tahnn and Weave technology to scan it.

The Tahnn computers did the rest.

They identified the Doctor.

So when this was reported back to the Tahnn Primary, he had to decide what to do. First he accessed the Tahnn databanks. Then those pirated from the Weave over the centuries. Then he even hacked into the Shadow Proclamation.

When he learned that even the Daleks had a unique name for the Doctor which suggested, if not fear, then a certain trepidation bordering on respect, the Primary made his decision.

The Doctor was trouble.

The Tahnn had a mission.

The two were not necessarily mutually incompatible.

'Bring the plan forward,' he declared to his advisers. 'Ignore protocol. Ignore the safeguards. Destroy the Weave and this Doctor as soon as we have confirmed the Weave location. Our agent suspects where the Weave ship is. The presence of the Doctor would seem to confirm that. Protocol be damned – blast that whole area into space dust.'

One of his advisers, an experienced campaigner who had assisted many Tahnn commanders over the years, ventured to suggest that High Command on Tahnnis might not agree to this incursion and that reportage homewards was a good idea. 'Just so they know what we are planning and why we have deviated from the plan.'

The adviser stopped breathing at that point, somewhat forcibly and – for him at least – unexpectedly. The Primary wondered if anyone else in his team of advisers had anything to add.

Curiously, none did.

And so after eons of waiting, the Tahnn ship dropped out of hiding and began a slow but sure move towards the third planet in the solar system.

Chapter
12

The sun was setting on a busy day.

The Doctor was in his shirt sleeves, sat in a striped deckchair in the rear garden, positioned by the French doors that led into the dining room. He was reading.

Oliver Marks and Rory were playing chess by the willow tree.

Amy was pacing a lot, and Rory reckoned she was anxious to sort out this Tahnn problem and get back into the TARDIS and go.

Oliver put Rory into check again.

'That's the eleventh game, Rory. Give up, mate,' the Doctor offered sagely.

Amy sighed. 'Why aren't we doing anything, Doctor?' she whined.

The Doctor held up a thick blue book. 'Reading, Amy. Learning.'

She wandered over to him and leant over the back of his chair, resting her chin on his head. 'Wotcha reading, mister?'

'Enola Porter's notebooks. Fascinating stuff.'

'Boooooring,' Amy said and went and sat on the small step by the French doors. 'You used to be more thrilling,' she muttered.

The Doctor gave her a curious look, shrugged, and returned to his reading, absorbing everything he could about Enola Porter's life and experiences.

Enola Porter, it seemed, had always been a strong-willed girl. Her various governesses and maids had always said she was a handful. Her parents had often despaired of her – no frilly dresses and bonnets for the young Enola; no dolly's tea parties or pony rides in Hyde Park on a Sunday. For Enola Tucker, at the age of 8, had discovered the stories of Rider Haggard, Conan Doyle and Jules Verne. Tales of high derring-do and adventure, with strong, intelligent men protecting young women of spunk and smarts who could quite easily have coped without their male 'heroes'.

Enola had lived through the war, witnessed the departure of the *Titanic*, experienced the Great Depression, all forming important parts of her development, so her interest in 'events' was always piqued. Her family never shielded her from the world, for they could see it was pointless and, after her mother had died of influenza, her father gave in to his daughter's wilful demands. Instead of being sent to some finishing school in Europe, Enola had been allowed to accompany her eccentric Uncle Bertie to the Dark Continent, the Far East and the Americas while her father remained in London, making a good living as a banker and helping finance her trips.

It had been Uncle Bertie who'd unwittingly piqued her interest in exploration and archaeology. He'd taken her to Vienna, ostensibly to see the museum, but rather than look at old paintings and Austrian sculpture, Enola had attended a lecture given by Howard Carter. She'd stood and listened to Carter's passion for his subject, admiring his power and his sheer joy for life.

Years later, as she researched his life, she would come to learn of the great sadness that permeated much of his success, of friends lost and the hardships involved in getting backers to support his expeditions. Although now universally famed for the Egyptian discoveries his team had made, Carter was more than a one-trick pony, and Enola always believed that he would surely be disappointed that all his other achievements would be forever overshadowed by Tutankhamun.

When he'd tried to drag her to see some Renaissance painting or other, Uncle Bertie had recognised that her real interest was in discovery and science. He had tried to explain this to her father, but he'd never truly understood. Or cared much.

Never recovering from the torture of his wife dying so painfully in his arms in 1919, Mr Tucker was quite happy to let Enola do whatever she wanted. It was as if all his love of life had been extinguished when he lost Enola's mother.

'Just don't let your heart be broken by love.' That had been his last, embittered, advice before she and Uncle Bertie had headed to Peking to begin an attempt to follow Marco Polo's route through the Far East. Although she rarely listened to her father (frankly she rarely listened to anyone), this thing about not getting emotionally involved with anyone had stuck with her and, while Uncle Bertie flitted from pretty young girl to pretty young girl like a forgetful butterfly, Enola had never allowed anyone to enter her emotional sphere. As a result, she had many friends but no constant companions.

When Uncle Bertie was shot and killed by an itinerant in a Moroccan bazaar, she briefly thought of returning home to her father. But, at Bertie's funeral, Marten Heinke had made his presence known and, before long, Enola was on her way back to Great Britain to find out about a burial mound that had been researched but remained unexcavated in Norfolk. There she had met the recently widowed Nathaniel Porter and, despite a few grumbles from the locals, had rapidly found herself becoming his new bride, a fact that had surprised her even more than it had the residents of Shalford Heights. For she doubted she truly loved him, and vice versa. But somehow they completed one another, provided what the other actually needed. This wasn't a lover or even a friend, but a partner, a respectable person, whose arm she could hold at social parties and whose friends and family seemed so distant and far away as to not be bothered with such things as love and weddings. Indeed, Enola couldn't quite remember if her father had even come up from London for the wedding.

That was odd, the Doctor thought. Why couldn't she remember that?

Anyway, after the marriage, Nathaniel Porter was very keen for his new wife to begin her work on the burial mound found along with the fogou beneath the school grounds. Much to the consternation of some of the locals, Porter had managed to get permission to have the school closed for the summer months and the grounds churned up. First Enola had contacted a man she had briefly met in Ceylon, Hamish Ridley, who agreed to join the team, eager to learn more about a hitherto unknown warrior buried in the English countryside.

Ridley's presence had proven trickier to arrange than Enola had anticipated – at some point he had come into a 'dispute' (his word, it seemed) with the authorities. Specifically, the Customs and Excise had seemed to suggest that Ridley had previously caused some 'affair' over something he had brought back from Marrakesh once that may or may not have been his to bring back.

Ridley was a charmer and very sophisticated, although Enola remained immune to his charms. She needed a good geologist and experienced excavator, and so her new husband had used his not inconsiderable influence (it always surprised Enola just how much influence he seemed to have) to get him into the country. Still, Hamish Ridley did spend a great deal of time looking over his shoulder, both metaphorically and quite literally, so Enola was never entirely sure how long it would be before someone turned up and carted him off to jail.

Christopher Maginn she had heard of but never met. She had read a number of his papers on British burial mounds, Stonehenge and that sort of thing. Stone circles weren't really Enola's interest, but the barrows at Avebury, Cornwall and especially West Kennet had always fascinated her. Maginn was another charmer, although she found his company less bearable – he was almost too suffocatingly friendly at times. He also quoted Oscar Wilde and chatted to the younger farmhands a little too much for her comfort. There were rumours about him and a young male archaeologist from Guildford, but then there were just as many stories about him and young girls working in pubs and factories, so it was difficult to know what to believe.

Then there had been old Walpole Spune – the strange man who believed in science and divination equally, who went to Church without fail on Sundays (except in Shalford Heights, where there wasn't one) but didn't cherish the Bible in way, shape or form, reckoning it was of no more historical relevance than the fairy tales of the Brothers Grimm. But he was fascinated by God, because of the way God united people and simultaneously set them at one another's throat. He had survived three wars and it was said he once saw the Angel of Mons, though Enola seemed not to have asked him about that. The Doctor reckoned Enola probably wasn't sure she could believe him, whatever his response. She clearly didn't like Spune that much – she thought him a coward, both intellectually and literally – but his enthusiasm couldn't be faulted. Ultimately, whatever the foibles of her team, they were all good at their jobs. Even Marten Heinke.

Sullen and almost rude to the point that she wanted to fire him, it was Heinke's brilliant artwork that kept him around. Neither she nor the other two men were especially great with cameras but Marten Heinke was more than capable of recording everything in his charcoals.

The most recent notebook entry implied that today was, theoretically, the day that her trowel would finally break through the mud and earth and chalk and grit – the day that she would finally break through into the burial chamber. To discover a warrior chieftain. Or a stone age family. Or Roman remains. Or any number of things that could have been placed there any time between 5000 BC and AD 900.

Sadly, despite everything she had written in her journals, right up to that very morning, the Doctor didn't believe anyone else would ever read a word of them, and he told Rory and Amy this.

'Her life is fascinating, but she is obsessed by this burial mound.'

Rory reached down into Enola's satchel and produced a crumpled sheet of paper. 'Why do you think she put this in there?'

The Doctor regarded the paper. It was the sketch that Marten Heinke had drawn earlier of him and Rory, both in the wrong clothes, and with woolly heads. 'Because she knew I'd nick her bag. Because she wanted me to have it.'

'Why?' Rory asked. 'The German guy's a bit surly and an imaginative artist, but not scary.'

The Doctor passed Rory and Amy one of the other books. 'There's a picture tucked in between 1922 and 1923. For safekeeping – I don't think the dates are significant. More a way of ensuring none of her current team find it.'

Amy unfurled the paper they found in the book. It was another Marten original. But this one showed a wedding scene – the Porters' wedding, in fact. The wedding wasn't in a church; it was clearly where the dig was taking place – the schoolyard, directly above the burial chamber. And every single guest at the wedding had woollen faces except four. Her,

Maginn, Ridley and Nathaniel Porter. The three archaeologists looked normal. The bridegroom however was… bizarre, even for a Marten Heinke sketch.

He had three heads. His own recognisable one, a formless woollen one and a blank, almost shapeless one.

'Three heads, only one of them human,' Amy said.

'Imaginative,' the Doctor said again. 'And a bit too Hieronymus Bosch for me.'

Rory tapped the picture. 'Enola's not scared of Marten Heinke, Doctor. She's scared of her husband.'

'Spot on,' said the Doctor. 'I wonder why.'

'Because she thinks he's going to kill her,' said Oliver Marks, apparently dozing by the abandoned chess game. But clearly not.

'Why?'

Oliver waved in the general direction of the picture Amy was holding. 'Because one morning a few weeks ago, she saw him heading to the kitchen in the Manse. When she called to him, he turned and looked at her. And just for a split second, she apparently saw those three heads on his shoulders.'

'She told you that?' asked Amy. 'Why?'

'She trusts me,' Oliver said simply. 'I don't know why. Maybe she was spooked and needed a confidant.'

The Doctor slammed the books to the ground.

'I'm a fool. But Enola Porter isn't. Well, she is, because she's opening that burial mound and knows damn well what's in there and how dangerous it is to her. She doesn't know how dangerous it is to the whole world, obviously, but that's not the point.'

Amy shrugged. 'The light in the Manse isn't great. And maybe this picture put that image into her head and she saw it in her imagination.'

'Well, you would say that. You need Enola to gain access to the ship.'

'What?' said Amy.

'Well, you're not really Amy Pond, are you, let's be honest.'

'What do you mean she's not Amy?' demanded Rory.

'Blimey, Rory, your marriage is not gonna be good if you can't even tell which Amy is which.' He looked at Amy. 'Where is she?'

'I don't understand,' Amy protested, but Rory grabbed her arm.

'OK, I get it now. I had my suspicions earlier, your disinterest, the pheasant and thinking the Doctor came from Mars. Now I know for sure. The real Amy wouldn't just dismiss something like a three-headed creature in an English village in 1936!'

'Good boy, Rory,' said the Doctor. 'I thought you hadn't got it.'

'You knew for how long?'

'Well, I sort of guessed when you did. The Mars thing was a dead giveaway actually. The real Amy sending us a message, I think. She's smart, that one.'

'Well, I'm glad you take it so easily. Of course, as far as I know, Amy being exchanged for fake Amys happens all the time for you.'

'No, actually. First time, I think.'

'For me too, so sorry if I didn't run round making accusations that could've made me look foolish in front of my fiancé!' Rory stared at Amy 'But God, it's a good copy.'

Amy smiled. 'Thank you.'

Rory took a deep breath. 'Why are you here? I mean, who are you exactly?'

'She's one of the Weave, Rory,' the Doctor said quietly. 'Which means Amy is safe because they need to keep the originals alive and well.' He touched Rory's arm gently. 'We'll get her back safely. Promise.'

Rory looked like he was about to argue, but he held back.

The Doctor looked at the fake Amy. 'We'll ask this politely, just once more. Who are you?'

'Like you care,' said the fake Amy.

That wasn't a reaction anyone had expected.

'What do you mean?'

'You abandoned me,' she snapped.

The Doctor was wrong-footed immediately. 'What? What? Why are you saying that?'

'You abandoned me,' she repeated. 'For years.'

'What, in Leadworth?' he said, remembering the

fourteen years Amy had waited for him. 'I said I was sorry…'

'Not Leadworth,' she said. 'Here.'

'I never abandoned you here. We've haven't even been here a day yet.'

'Six thousand years we have waited for you,' Amy said. 'Six. Thousand. Years.' She smacked him hard across the face. 'You abandoned me here six thousand years ago!'

The Doctor suddenly recalled his visit to the Weave world all those lives ago. The little girl he'd taken to see the universe. The little girl he'd given a TARDIS homing beacon to. The little girl he'd befriended.

'It can't be you. You're all grown up!'

'We crashed here six thousand years ago. Just before we crashed, I set off your device, because you promised you'd come if ever I used it.'

'We did. The TARDIS picked it up,' the Doctor said. Then he sighed. 'But the signal bounced all the way through the time vortex and brought us to 1936 instead of when you crashed. Because something else nearby, in cosmic terms, is transmitting a signal and that interfered. I'm sorry. What do they call you on the ship? What's your position?'

'I am 6011.'

The Doctor did a swift calculation – so either side of you 3715, next up, 9726?'

6011 nodded.

'Fibonacci system, see, Rory? Well, sort of.

Anyway, I was right.'

'Yes, great, that helps Amy, Doctor. Look 6011 or whatever your name is, why do you need access to your ship?' Rory asked. 'You must have it already.'

6011 shrugged. 'I don't understand the question.'

'Everything your people have done,' said the Doctor, 'has been gearing towards getting Enola Porter to access your ship. But that's mad, because you can clearly come and go as you please.'

'They are coming,' Oliver yelled suddenly.

'Not now, Olly,' muttered the Doctor, but 6011 was distracted.

'He senses the Tahnn?'

'Ignore him. Please. This is important. Why do you need Enola Porter to get to your ship?'

'I don't know what you are talking about. We are hiding from the Tahnn. We, too, can sense they are coming.'

'That's what he keeps saying,' Rory jerked his head back at the distraught Oliver Marks.

'And he's right,' 6011 said. 'The Tahnn are close, so we are hiding among the villagers, trying to keep an eye out.'

'So the Librarian, the farmer, Marten Heinke, I presume?'

'Yes. People to keep an eye out. 41200, the one you know as Marten, has been trying to warn people away from the ship. The *Exalted* must be protected at all costs.' 6011 was getting anxious now. 'We must get back to my Commander. This man can sense the Tahnn. His mind has been touched by them. He is the beacon, drawing them ever closer.'

'Don't even think about hurting him,' said Rory angrily.

'But they must not find the ship,' 6011 said desperately.

'I don't understand,' said Rory. 'If these Tahnn want to destroy you, why don't they just blast this place? Oliver is apparently giving off waves telling them where you are. If I were them, I'd just zap away.'

The Doctor was staring at Rory, mouth agape.

'Sorry,' Rory said. 'I just thought—'

'No, you are brilliant!' The Doctor said. 'They want the ship. They want the crew dead but the reason they've not destroyed anything yet is they want what's in the ship, yes?'

6011 nodded. 'Of course, they want the Glamour. That's what we are protecting! That's why that archaeologist woman must not be permitted to get access. The moment she breaks the walls of the ship, the Glamour will escape into the atmosphere. And the Tahnn will siphon it up and have it.'

'What's the Glamour?' asked Rory.

The Doctor clicked his fingers. 'Your family mentioned that to me, all those years ago. It's important to you, isn't it?'

'It's why the Tahnn warred with us. We had the Glamour naturally. They wanted it, to use it as a weapon, to create confusion rather than ecstasy.'

'Walked right into this with eyes wide closed,' the Doctor said, suddenly angry. 'Stupid Doctor. Stupid, stupid Doctor. Why didn't I see this earlier, Rory? I was suspicious but not suspicious enough.'

'What are you talking about?'

'Who keeps Olly here as a beacon to the Tahnn. Who married an archaeologist to ensure she got to the Weave ship? Who has the ability to become a copy of Daisy taken from an old photo to throw us off the scent? And who couldn't read the psychic paper and must immediately have known we were alien?'

Rory nodded. 'Nathaniel Porter? He's a Tahnn?'

'Must be.'

'Can't be.'

'Why not?'

Rory pointed at Oliver Marks. 'Because he keeps saying they are coming not that they are already here. If Nathaniel Porter was a Tahnn, surely he'd sense it?'

'Oh, Rory!'

'What?'

'I hate it when you're right. But there's something strange about Nathaniel Porter.' He turned to 6011. 'Your people, like you've done with Amy, you download their memories when you copy them, yes?'

'Short-term memory, basic characteristics and so on, yes.'

'Rory, what did Olly tell us? That the villagers had left over the last few years. So, Nathaniel Porter needs an archaeologist. Meantime, Mrs Porter thinks, "My husband's a bit weird." Maybe she finds out the truth – bingo, under the patio for her, as Amy – real Amy – mentioned earlier. So rather than just getting an archaeologist in, he marries one. Long-term plan, but other people spot the differences, so he gets rid of them, forces them to move out – he can't kill them or he starts to look like Dr Crippen – apart from a few people still loyal to him out of long-time respect. The Porters have run this place for years, remember.'

'So if he's not a human, and he's not a Tahnn, what is he?' Rory asked.

'That's easy,' the Doctor said. He looked at 6011. 'I assume the reason you can't just take off, other than the ethics of wiping out a village in the back-blast, is because your ship depends on all twenty-five sequential crew being present, yeah?'

6011 in Amy's body nodded.

'And you don't have a full complement, do you?'

'No, two of the crew died in the crash, and two more have disappeared subsequently.'

'Who?'

'Our Executive Officer, 3, and our Tactical Officer, 25463. 3 disappeared shortly after we awoke. 25463 went to retrieve him about ten years later.'

'Ten years? Blimey,' said Rory.

'In a species as long lived as the Weave, Rory, ten years is an afternoon to you. So one of those two was working for the Tahnn, to supply them with the Glamour. Probably long before you crashed.'

6011 gasped. 'Before we crashed, when I sent your TARDIS homing beacon out into space, I met 3 walking around our ship. I was surprised, because he should have been overseeing the hibernation chambers.'

'So 3 finds himself taking on the life of Nathaniel Porter, because that's a great way to ensure no one questions anything you do, while secretly bringing the Tahnn here, using Oliver there as a guiding light.'

Rory nodded. 'Just like you said he was.'

6011 was shaking her head. 'No Weave would ever betray a ship to the Tahnn, least of all one carrying the Glamour.'

'Your faith is touching,' said the Doctor, 'but I reckon it's misplaced.'

Rory was walking over to Oliver Marks, who was staring dead ahead again, back in the throes of a flashback.

'Oliver, it's Rory. How long have you felt them coming? How often do you sense, smell and taste the Tahnn?'

'Every day,' Oliver breathed. 'Every single day.'

Rory threw a look at the Doctor. 'Doctor, I'm not going to pretend to be an expert in this spacey stuff, but what if there's a third option.' He took Oliver's hand. 'Every day you say? Every day since Daisy died?'

Oliver tried to speak but couldn't at first, his mind battling with the question. Then he shook his head. 'No. No, only since... since...'

'Since Mrs Porter brought you to recuperate in Shalford Heights, where she thought you'd be safe. Not realising her husband had manipulated her into doing it. And once you were here, you could smell the Tahnn, yes? Hear them? Feel them?'

'Yes. Here. I can feel them coming. Here!'

'No you can't, Oliver. I'm sorry, but you are wrong. Because if you had sensed them coming over the last six or so years, they'd be here by now, wouldn't they?'

Oliver wanted to reply but couldn't. The logic Rory had thrown at him panicked him.

'Doctor, Oliver was wrong and because we believed him, we're wrong. The Tahnn aren't coming.'

'You mean, it's all wrong? Oliver couldn't sense them at all?'

'No, not at all. It's the PTSD – he doesn't know what he's actually sensing. His logical mind kept saying it had to be the Tahnn coming. But he was wrong. The reason he can sense them every day? It's because they are already here. They always have been. That's why he senses them. The Tahnn are already here in Shalford Heights and have been here even longer than Oliver.'

The Doctor gave a 'Yes!' very loudly. 'Rory, you are more magnificent than I thought you were before.' He looked at Rory. 'I've said that a lot lately, like I expected you to be a bit dim. I'm sorry, I had no right to treat you that way.'

Rory shrugged. 'It's all right. Let's get Amy back safely and I'll forgive you.'

'Oh, Amy's fine, isn't she, 6011?'

'Absolutely.' The Weave smiled at Rory. 'She loves you an awful lot, I can tell you that.'

Rory blushed. 'Anyway,' he said, 'what if Nathaniel Porter is a Tahnn-Weave hybrid.'

'Impossible,' said 6011. 'No Weave would allow their body to be defiled in such a way.'

'Well, as theories go, that's a bit of a leap, Rory,' said the Doctor. 'Which is why I like it. And it explains everything.' He looked hard at 6011. 'You had a cuckoo in the nest.'

'But if a Tahnn has access to Weave physiology, it could be anyone. We have no Tahnn prisoner in the ship, so we wouldn't know who 3 was pretending to be.'

'Do you have the real Nathaniel Porter?'

'Of course not.'

The Doctor shrugged. 'I bet he never survived the meeting with your double agent. So, Tahnns are basically humanoid, going by Oliver's description, bar the prune faces. So let's say two arms, two legs, heart, lungs, etc, yes?'

'If you say so,' said Rory.

'The Weave, however, are vastly different. They look like wool, but in fact it's a marvellous form of flexible protein ribbons, always in flux. So they can interconnect with one another, their technology and so on. The ship and crew are all one living organism – when one dies, they're all in trouble.'

Rory considered this. 'So if Nathaniel Porter is a Tahnn with the capabilities of a Weave…'

'He's about the most dangerous thing on this planet right now.' The Doctor turned to stare crossly at 6011. 'And you, you and your people brought him here and never realised. I thought you were better than that. What happened to all that peace and prosperity and stuff I remember?'

'It died during the war with the Tahnn.' 6011 started to walk away.

'Oi, I haven't finished yet.'

'That's irrelevant. I need to take this information back to my Commander and make sure Enola Porter does not break through the hull of our ship.'

Rory frowned. 'Your ship can fly through outer space, but a woman with a trowel can damage it?'

'They are four Weave down, Rory,' the Doctor explained. 'That's like you having pneumonia – all your defences are down. Their ship is very sick and prone to deterioration.'

6011 snatched up the two drawings that Marten Heinke had done showing Weave heads on human bodies. 'Maybe these will remind Enola what she is up against,' 6011 said and walked away.

Rory sighed. 'She still looks like Amy to me.'

The Doctor was settling Oliver in his chair. 'We need to get him safely inside.'

'Why?'

'Because the moment Enola damages that ship, the rest of the Tahnn will be here, and Nathaniel Porter, or whatever hybrid he is, will no longer need Olly alive. Place him inside with Old John and the other staff; he should be safe for a bit.'

'Unless our space killers just think it expedient to kill everyone in the house en masse.'

'Oh, you are Mr Cheerful today, Rory Williams. Come on, we need to catch up with her!'

Chapter
13

Not far away, just beneath the school rugby pitch, Enola Porter and her band of archaeologists were preparing for the momentous occasion. Enola and Christopher Maginn were posing for a quick sketch by Marten Heinke, who was more nervous than normal. Hamish Ridley and Walpole Spune were checking their equipment.

'I live for moments like this,' said Ridley. 'You?'

Spune just shrugged. 'I've seen enough things in my lifetime. One more is neither here nor there.'

'Gosh, you're cheerful, aren't you.' Ridley shook his head.

'Enola,' said Marten, putting down his artwork. 'I must ask you again not to do this.'

Enola laughed. 'Why, for heaven's sake?'

'You know why,' he said darkly. 'I have shown you enough times in my drawings.'

'What's he talking about, Enola?' asked Maginn, but she waved him away.

'Let me discuss this with Marten privately, Christopher,' she said. 'Can you go and stop Spune and Hamish from assaulting one another, yes?'

With a dismissive sigh, Maginn did as bidden.

Enola grabbed Marten's arm. 'Who are you really?'

'I am Marten Heinke.'

'You most certainly are not. Oh, you have his talent and his attitude off pat, but the Marten I first met would not have drawn woolly faces on people. You tried to warn me about my husband and about the Doctor, didn't you?'

'I have to stop you, Enola. I allowed this charade to continue because I needed to stay undercover, not reveal myself. I had hoped I could scare you away from this path.'

She snorted. 'If you knew me at all, you'd have realised very early on – the more you push me away, the more I push forward. What is behind this wall of mud? What are you hiding?'

'You wouldn't believe me if I told you.'

'Try me. The Doctor reckoned it was something unearthly, a spaceship or something. I think he might be right. You're not human, are you, Marten?'

Marten regarded her carefully and actually smiled. 'You are an exceptional human being, Enola.

I am honoured to have known you. But if you don't leave this dig now, you will not survive what is to come.'

'And what's that?'

'A race of aliens called the Tahnn. They want what is inside our ship.'

'Your... I see.' Enola glanced over at the other three. 'Are they with you?'

Marten looked affronted. 'No of course not. As if!'

Enola laughed cheerfully. 'I admire your honesty. But I need a stronger reason not to discover your ship than you simply asking me not to.'

Marten pulled her closer. 'If you damage our hull, you will release something... something I can't put into words that a human can understand. A concept, an energy field. We call it the Glamour. It can change... reality.'

Enola's eyes glittered. 'And you want me to fail to find that?'

'The human race is not... genetically conditioned to control it. Your world could go mad, literally insane, in moments.'

Enola considered that. 'But I want to understand that. Can you not see? You know my life – it's been building up to this moment.'

'Then be the better woman,' said Marten. 'For the sake of your species and mine, abort this. Please. I promise you, my people can show you wonders, anything. But don't damage our ship. It is so weak after centuries underground, undernourished and damaged.'

Enola looked at Marten and thought of the drawings he'd done.

He nodded. 'I can guess what you are thinking. But imagine if I had come to you and said, "Hallo, I am an alien pretending to be your Germanic friend and I want you to leave my spaceship alone." You'd have thought I was mad.'

'Why do you assume I don't think that now?'

Marten shrugged. 'Because I am desperate. And I hope you understand that.'

They were disturbed by a shout from Ridley and Spune, fighting over something.

'My divination drew us here,' Spune was insisting.

'Nonsense,' countered Ridley. 'You can't divine a dig. Research, historical writings and a damn good leader in Enola Porter brought us here.'

'Careful lads,' Enola started, but Walpole Spune was having none of it. 'You are so closed-minded, Ridley. Have you not seen how marvellous the world is? There's room for all aspects of science.'

'Waving a blasted stick above the ground and saying you've found water, oil, money or the ruddy burial site of an Iron Age chieftain is not science. It's rubbish!'

Which was when Walpole Spune, frustrated at not being taken seriously at a moment of great discovery, shoved Hamish Ridley really hard into the wall. The wall between the archaeologists and the *Exalted*.

The wall caved in. Earth and mud and stone poured down.

Enola could only watch in shock as, for a tiny moment, she saw the alien spaceship beyond. It looked like a massive lump of green wool – that was the only way she could think of it.

That tiny moment ended as Hamish Ridley fell into the spaceship. Through it. Ripping an enormous gash in its side.

'No!' screeched Marten, or whoever he really was, behind her.

'Blimey,' was Christopher Maginn's comment.

''Pon my soul,' was Walpole Spune's.

If Hamish Ridley said anything as he fell into the ship, it was drowned out by the vast roar of something that seemed to come from within the ship. No, not from within, Enola realised. It was more like a yell of pain that came from the actual walls. And from Marten, behind her.

The noise didn't stop. It grew louder. Then a massive sparkling luminous burst of green-yellow energy poured out of the fresh rent, bathing them all.

This, Enola realised, was not light. It was something more. She felt it reach into her body, into the very molecules that made her exist, running through them, through the billions of atomic gaps in her cell structure.

To her, it just felt like someone had looked into her soul.

She blacked out.

6011 gasped in pain as she reached the road leading to the school.

'No,' she hissed, 'I'm too late.'

'Indeed you are, 6011,' said a chilling voice behind her.

She turned and faced what she only knew as Nathaniel Porter. 'You traitor,' she said. 'You betrayed the Commander, the Weave, everything.'

'Not at all,' said Nathaniel Porter. 'I can't betray what I never believed in, can I?'

His face blurred and changed, and 6011 saw its Weave form adopt its true Weave features.

'You!' she gasped.

'Me,' he replied reaching out to grab her shoulders. 'The Glamour is going to be mine,' he said, and let his body turn to wool, flowing into 6011's. She couldn't scream. She could do nothing as the powerful man literally tore her apart, strand by strand. She had no time to think of anything until, in her very last moment of life, she remembered being happy. Being a child back home. Going on a voyage of discovery.

The TARDIS. The suns and moons and stars. The space-time vortex. The Doctor with a different face, smiling as he showed her the wonders that the universe possessed.

And 6011 died thinking back to the one good memory she could muster.

For a moment, Nathaniel Porter was pure Weave, then he drew what was left of 6011's body into himself, feeding off it. The next moment he transformed into a red-suited warrior, sallow-faced and oily-breathed. And then he was Nathaniel Porter again.

'The Glamour belongs to the Tahnn,' he said to himself.

Inside the Manse, Old John was sitting with Oliver Marks in his rooms, as the Doctor had asked him to.

The disturbed former soldier was lying on his bed, shivering, eyes open, staring up at the ceiling but seeing... seeing something Old John could only hope he would never experience himself.

Somehow the limping old man knew the Weave ship had been ruptured.

Because for a moment, everything became clear to him.

Because, in his mind's eye, he was 14 again. When he had snuck out from his father's homestead, in the dark, and investigated the torn-open ground where the Sky Gods had sent their emissary.

He had entered that hole, feeling his way in the dark, until he touched it.

It wasn't rock, or iron or anything hard. It was soft, springy.

He had pushed against it, feeling it give, and then, somehow, his right foot had found a weak spot, like a knot in wood. He had massaged at it, worked at it until it gave way, and as first his foot then his leg had pushed into the weakened area of whatever it was he was exploring, he had heard a terrible noise. A screech of pain. A roar of anger.

He was bathed in a momentary green light and flung back.

The breach had sealed itself.

The green glow was gone.

He had tried to get up, but his leg was shattered. So was his ankle, his foot and each toe.

And he had begun screaming until the whole village woke and managed to find him. Tor and his father Wulf had been horrified.

'Owain,' they'd said. 'Owain, what have you done to displease the Sky Gods so?'

But the Sky Gods were not displeased, it seemed. No crops failed, no herds died. Indeed, for the rest of the village, life had carried on as normal.

But for Owain, one thing wasn't normal. Because his father died at the age of 35, and Tor died at 38, and his mother died at 29 (all good ages), but Owain himself didn't die. One by one, the villagers died as they would normally do, but he didn't. He just kept ageing, his leg never truly healing until he reached 65 years. His own children had had children by then. All had since died.

After 300 years, Owain knew this was the curse

the Sky Gods had given him. He lived on through so many hundreds of lives, changing his identity between Owain, Owen, Ian, Iain, Ewan, Euan and John – all variants of the same name – on a regular basis. Often he would leave what eventually grew into Shalford Heights for a generation, so he could return when no one would remember the old man with the bad limp who had once lived there.

But he knew why he was there. It was a punishment. For he had disturbed the gift of the Sky Gods, and his penance was to ensure that no other human did the same thing.

Over the centuries, of course, Owain learned to realise this had been no gift of the Sky Gods. There were no Sky Gods, not in the sense that Wulf and Tor had envisaged. Yet what was under that mound, whatever it was, had to be protected.

That was why he stayed in Shalford Heights and why, for the last twelve years, he had been employed by Nathaniel Porter.

And only he knew the truth.

One day he had followed Nathaniel Porter to the school, hoping he wasn't going near the mound. But he was. And Owain, by this time, known locally as Old John, had watched as creatures emerged from under the ground. Like woollen toys, man-sized and eager, first one then more had emerged from the ground. And, after a while, one on its own.

Nathaniel Porter had witnessed this too. Nathaniel Porter had approached this solitary creature and tried to speak to it. And it had devoured him. One moment Nathaniel Porter had been trying to talk to the wool creature, the next, he was wrapped within wool himself and then, his body was gone. A moment later the wool creature had become Nathaniel Porter.

Old John had limped back to the Manse, to warn Mrs Porter, but she wasn't there and he had never seen her again.

Nathaniel Porter, apparently saddened by the disappearance of his wife, had eventually declared her dead, and the rest had become a nightmare.

When Oliver Marks had arrived, Old John took to looking after him, much as he'd sworn to look after the gift of the Sky Gods. He had failed in that task. He would not fail Oliver Marks.

Except now, it would appear, he had.

Because Old John's leg seared in agony suddenly, and he knew. He knew the thing under the ground had been disturbed, and he cried out.

But Oliver Marks cried out more. One word, shrieked so loudly, it could probably be heard in London.

'Daisy!'

The door to the room was flung open, and the Doctor and Rory Williams and Amy Pond were standing there.

'I'm sorry,' wailed Old John. 'I'm so sorry.'

Oliver Marks sat bolt upright.

'They are here,' he announced to the four of them.

'I can smell them in the air.'

'Not yet they're not, Olly. Unless...' The Doctor stopped and looked at Rory and Amy. 'Oh very clever, we all fell for that.'

'What?' asked Rory.

'That's not Amy,' the Doctor said.

'I know,' said Rory. 'It's 6011.'

'No, it's not,' the Doctor said. '6011 may well be dead. He probably killed her.'

'Who?'

The Doctor threw his arms up in anguish. 'The person who isn't here. The person under our noses from the very beginning.'

Rory twigged just in time. He ducked away from 'Amy' as she shimmered and rewove herself into Nathaniel Porter.

Porter grinned. 'Too late, Doctor. The Glamour is mine. And now it is time to embrace it.' He dropped his human disguise altogether, weaving again, this time into a copy of his original form, a Tahnn officer. 'The perfect spy,' he said simply.

Oliver hid his face in his hands and began sobbing uncontrollably, and Rory was beside him in a second, trying to comfort him.

'When did you infiltrate the Weave?' demanded the Doctor

'Oh, three years before they crashed on Earth,' the Tahnn said.

'But you are one of the Weave,' Rory said. 'Tahnn can't do what you do.'

'The Tahnn studied them for centuries. Do you really believe our science couldn't find a way of replicating their physical structure? I was a guinea pig, a volunteer who could have lived or died. I am the first Tahnn super-soldier, built to infiltrate and kill.'

'You… you were my friend…' said Old John, aghast.

'No,' the alien laughed. 'But you were willing to believe I was. The human mind is so easy to manipulate.'

'What about the Glamour?' asked the Doctor. 'How will you operate it?'

The Tahnn laughed at him. 'The Glamour isn't a device, Doctor. It's an ideal. A reimagining of life. A reshaping of reality.'

The corridor behind them all was suddenly filled with green sparkling light, that seemed almost alive as it wove around, as if searching for something.

Rory wasn't entirely sure what happened next. This was mainly because the Doctor turned and threw himself at Rory and Old John, sending all three of them crashing to the ground.

Rory saw what looked like the air around them shimmer, like the haze of a mirage on the horizon, but close up.

He was aware of Oliver yelling close by and, in the corner of the room, the Tahnn soldier that had variously been Nathaniel Porter and Amy Pond seemed to just float into a billion particles, a look of pure surprise on his face as he simply dissipated out of existence.

Then Rory's view was utterly blanketed by the Doctor's body dropping over his face...

Chapter
14

In space, the Tahnn ship was approaching planet Earth. The Primary barked orders, more out of fear than anything else, most of them unnecessary because the crew were well trained.

One of his advisers stepped up. 'Sir, we have lost contact with our agent.'

'Explain.'

'His life signs, they just… stopped.'

Another adviser piped up. 'Primary. I'm reading a massive surge in energy on the planet. It… it's Weave energy, sir.'

'Has the fool activated the Glamour before we got there?'

'Impossible to tell, sir. But it is being controlled… somehow.'

The Primary frowned. 'The Weave? They are supposed to be fractured, unable to control any of their technology…'

'No, sir, it's not the Weave. It's… it's a human!'

'Impossible!' The Primary stood up and pushed both advisers aside. 'You idiots cannot read the equipment properly.'

Then a voice spoke to them. Spoke to every Tahnn aboard the ship: the Primary, his advisers, his soldiers, his cooks and even his janitors. Every single Tahnn on the ship heard the voice.

'I can sense you,' said the voice. 'I can smell you, I can feel you and, oh my goodness, for the first time, it feels right. It is time to move on, to change my life for good.'

The Primary stared at his crew.

'I no longer want to feel, smell, hear, or sense you in any way,' said the voice. 'So I won't.'

Before the Primary could utter a single word, he, his crew and his ship, simply dissolved into molecules that drifted on the solar winds and then were gone for ever.

Chapter
15

He felt strange, like his body was thrashing about under its own volition, like he had no control over any part of it, but that quickly stopped and all he could feel then was the Doctor lying on him, breathing deeply.

After a moment, the Doctor moved. 'Rory, you OK?'

'I think so,' he replied. 'You?'

'Don't know,' the Doctor said. 'Don't know about anything any more.' He got up and sloped away, leaving Rory to look around.

What had previously been Oliver Marks's rather dingy set of rooms was now a beautifully ornate room with a grand piano in one corner. There were paintings on the wall of people Rory didn't recognise and shelves of what he could only guess were extremely expensive books. The tatty carpet had given way to polished floorboards he could see his face reflected in.

'Doctor?'

'I know, Rory,' was the response from the room's only other occupant.

The Doctor was standing by the French doors, which no longer looked out on slightly overgrown and unkempt greenery but instead on beautifully cut lawns, striped and with beautiful borders of flowers. A small fountain was in the centre and at the far ends where the fence had been giving way was now a gazebo and a high brick wall.

'The big willow tree's the same,' Rory said, joining him. 'So we've not travelled in time.'

'What makes you so sure...' the Doctor started, then looked at Rory as if, once again, noticing the young nurse actually had a brain. 'No, you're spot on. I missed that. Good one.' He patted Rory's shoulder.

'Maybe Amy's here,' Rory said. 'The real one, not one of these blasted Weave.'

The Doctor nodded slowly. 'I hope so.' Then he sniffed the air. 'Yeah, yeah, she probably is.'

'You don't think she is at all, do you?'

'Nope,' the Doctor confessed. 'Not remotely. That'd be too easy.' He swung round to face the rearranged room and yelled at it. 'Too easy by far. Come on, show yourself!' he bellowed.

'Is that wise?'

The Doctor paused then shook his head. 'Nope, probably not. Ever known me to be wise?'

'Well...'

'Really?' the Doctor sounded almost affronted. 'No one ever wants to be told they're wise, Rory. Unless they're 90 years old.'

'You are ten times that.'

'Don't spoil my fun,' the Doctor said. 'Oi! Come on. Don't keep us waiting—'

The Doctor stopped as the door opened and a woman walked in.

'Oh hello,' he smiled. 'I'm the Doctor.'

'I know,' she said.

Rory realised she was the subject of one of the paintings on the wall and nudged the Doctor to draw his attention to the image in the really rather posh frame.

'Pride of place above the fireplace.' The Doctor stared at the portrait, squinting as he read the nameplate. 'It's better than the photo they hung in the old hallway,' he said.

Rory watched as the Doctor looked back at the newcomer in the doorway, whose red dress was in danger of falling and revealing more than it should. He actually flushed with embarrassment and hoped the Doctor wouldn't notice, but the Time Lord was too busy offering the woman his hand.

'Mrs Porter, I presume.' He bowed slightly. 'An honour to make your acquaintance. We've... heard a lot about you. May I present Mr Rory Williams. My friend.'

Mrs Porter spared Rory no more than a cursory glance, immediately focusing her attention back on the Doctor and starting to ease him towards the door.

Behind his back, the Doctor was gesticulating madly to Rory, pointing up and making circular motions.

It took a second before Rory realised he wanted him to look at all the paintings in the room. Either that or he wanted him to run in a circle, but he doubted that somehow.

Then the Doctor and the mysterious Mrs Porter were gone.

Rory checked the big painting of her, and sure enough that was who it said she was, although it was curious that it still gave no first name. How many people, he wondered, have their portraits painted and are then forever known as Mrs Porter.

Rory hadn't been travelling with the Doctor as long as Amy, but he had picked a few things up in that time. He knew a clue when he saw it. What it meant, right now, he had no idea, but something in the back of his mind told him that this was important. It could just be an affectation, but that seemed unlikely. Certainly for 1936. And the tree certainly implied this was still 1936.

Which was another clue. Why? Everything else in the garden had changed. Oh, it was the same garden, all right – different gardening job, but the shape and size was the same. Just like this room. Same room, different contents.

Someone's idealised idea of what the Manse might have looked like in its glory days.

He wandered over to the other paintings, but none of the nameplates meant anything to him. Bar one. It was a small painting, which he hadn't even noticed at first because it was part of a triptych and was closed a bit, but when he opened it, a familiar face stared at out at him.

Amy Pond. Three Amy Ponds. The central one was as she was when he last saw her that morning, but looking very stern, as if the painter had caught her on a bad day. The left-hand one was Amy as he first ever saw her: about 8 years old, long red hair, freckles, holding an oddly shaped teddy bear that she had loved so much back then. On the right was another more recent Amy, but wearing white – ohmygod, wearing a wedding dress. A nice one, too.

He'd never seen the dress she'd chosen for their big day.

That was meant to have taken place by now. Before the Doctor re-entered her life. And Rory's life. And turned both their lives upside down.

Mr and Mrs Williams. Pond-Williams? Williams-Pond? Oh, the hours of discussion on that subject. Well, maybe not hours, actually; more like minutes. And not pretty minutes.

Best not go there.

So anyway, why was there a set of Amy portraits hidden away in a dark corner of a huge room in this Manse that wasn't the same Manse he'd been in five minutes ago?

He glanced back out through the French doors at the big tree. The only remnant of the Manse he knew. Why? He tried to imagine it from earlier today, Oliver Marks sat in his chair out there, fearing… the return of the mysterious *them*. His post-traumatic stress disorder causing him so much distress. But it wasn't Rory's field of expertise, not in any way. He simply didn't know how to treat it beyond basic TLC.

Why was the tree the same? Again that voice in the back of his head, telling him this was significant. Same with the pictures of Amy. The sort of clues the Doctor would see and solve in a moment.

Except he hadn't. He hadn't even noticed the tree till Rory had pointed it out.

That was weird.

Weirder still, Rory noted, was that the door out of the room was gone and in its place was just more wall. The French Doors now had curtains drawn across them. He wrenched them back, expecting to see the garden. The pagoda. The tree.

Blank wall.

No, not blank – a painting shimmered into existence in front of him.

A painting of a tree. Not the willow tree from

outside, though – this was an old greeny-yellowy tree, twisted roots above the ground. It was surrounded by others, but all blurred and out of focus, drawing attention to the main one.

'Great,' said Rory. 'Just what I needed.'

The Doctor walked along the polished, well-lit corridors of the Manse.

'Nice house,' he said. 'Yours?'

'In a way, Mr Doctor,' Mrs Porter replied, tossing her long blonde hair down across the back of her scarlet dress.

'Same layout, different coat of paint,' he said to his escort. 'Alternative world? Parallel reality? Sliding doors existence? Or just a straightforward illusion?'

'I have no knowledge of these things you speak of, Mr Doctor,' Mrs Porter said in a tone that suggested she really didn't. She picked up the hem of her blossoming white gown. 'We should hurry; our host is most anxious to greet you properly. He apologises that Chivers left you alone in the Withdrawing Room for so very long.'

'Chivers? Oh, right, the butler did it. And, obviously, I wasn't alone.'

'Really, sir? I saw no one with you.'

'Yes, you did. My second-best friend, Rory Williams. I introduced you to him.'

'I saw no one, sir,' said the enigmatic Mrs Porter.

The Doctor looked back the way they had walked

and noted that there was only darkness behind. 'Like someone's not just shutting off the light behind us, Mrs P, but the whole world.' He stopped walking suddenly and, after a few more steps, Mrs Porter did the same.

'We really must move quickly, Mr Doctor, sir,' she said, straightening the apron on her black maid's outfit.

'Three changes of attire in three beats, that's a new one on me,' the Doctor said. He grabbed her arm. 'Focus, Mrs Porter. Focus.'

She stared into his eyes, then closed hers, and the Doctor watched as the maid's outfit reassembled into the tight scarlet dress of earlier.

'Whoever is manipulating the Glamour hasn't quite mastered it yet. Their concentration keeps slipping.'

Mrs Porter shrugged. 'This way, Mr Doctor,' she said and pushed open a door that the Doctor knew had previously led into the old dining room.

It was now a lavishly decorated ballroom. The room was the same size as before, but every time the Doctor looked in a different direction or at different people and things, just out of the corner of his eye, the room adjusted itself, rearranged, reformed to imply it was bigger than it was.

'Think,' he said to himself.

In his mind's eye, he could see the whole room and all the people in it, but not in the way the room wanted him to see it. Now he saw it as it really *was*:

people and objects crammed together; a man in a nice suit, whose lower left leg was actually a small table, a lady sat on a chaise longue, although the lower half of her body was the chaise longue; and a young man in military uniform who seemed to be leaning against the fireplace, yet the whole right side of his body was actually the wall.

The Doctor closed his eyes, took a deep breath and allowed the unreality to flood into him again, and see the room, the furniture and the people as the room wanted to be seen. It was less confusing that way, and anyway he knew the reality now.

A man was seated at the piano, playing soundlessly.

'Nathaniel Porter?' the Doctor asked, guessing from the attentive way that the guests were hanging on his playing that he was their host.

The man turned. It wasn't Nathaniel Porter. It was Oliver Marks. Smiling.

'Doctor, you made it.'

'Just about, Olly. Not everything's quite as it was. Or should be.'

'That's to be expected,' Oliver said, standing. 'Doctor, there's someone I'd like you to meet. Don't think you've met her properly before.'

'Another lady, Oliver? I've already had the pleasure of meeting someone I assume is the missing first Mrs Porter. Who next?'

A young woman in a short flapper skirt, diadem around her head and hair bobbed into kiss curls around her cheeks was suddenly standing next to Oliver, holding his hand.

'My wife,' Oliver said. 'Doctor, meet Daisy Marks.'

Two children seemed to detach themselves from Daisy's legs. They couldn't have been hiding behind her but something was skewing the Doctor's perspective. Of course, they'd been there all along, he just hadn't seen them.

'Davey and Calleagh, meet the Doctor. A very old and valued friend,' Oliver said.

The Doctor closed his eyes, refocusing his mind – trying to bring back the reality he'd seen of jumbled people and things, flesh and inorganics melded as one, a jumble, a mishmash of concepts and ideas.

He opened his eyes.

Blast it, the room was still as he didn't want it to be – perfect. Now with added children shaking his hand and curtseying.

'Davey, Calleagh,' he found himself saying, though every fibre of his being resisted. Why? Why was he getting drawn into this mirage? He needed something... something to pull him back to reality.

The crowd was parting, almost reverentially, as someone made their way through. Now what?

And then, facing him, tall, flame-haired, but wearing a blue duffel coat with a little bobble cap and mittens... Amy Pond.

'Amy!'

'Is that my name, sir?' she asked. 'I wasn't sure.

Are you who I'm looking for?'

'Quite possibly, Amy, yes.'

'Are you the love of my life?' She held out her hand and the Doctor could see the engagement ring on it.

'No,' he said quietly. 'No, that's Rory. I think that may be who you are looking for. He's...' The Doctor went to wave in the direction of the hallway that Mrs Porter had led him down but it was gone. As was the door Amy had walked through. 'He's elsewhere,' the Doctor finished. 'Tell you what, why don't you stay here and I'll see if I can rustle him up for you.'

'Thank you,' Amy said dreamily.

'Quite like you quieter for once,' the Doctor said, but not meaning it at all. What he wanted back was his Amy. Sparky, feisty, smart and clever.

'Doctor, do you like my world?' asked Oliver Marks.

'Not especially, Olly. Bit chaotic for me.'

'I can't hear them any more,' Oliver said. 'I sent them away.'

'Did you? That's Glamour for you. Brings you exactly what you want and blow the consequences.'

'What consequences?' Oliver frowned. 'For the first time in ages, I feel brilliant.'

The Doctor tried to stop sounding exasperated. 'Yes, that's the problem with Glamour. The Weave tempted me with it once, but I said no because I knew it was fake. It's like a drug, Olly. OK, so it's not medically harmful, but none of this is real, and the comedown will probably be pretty dramatic when it fades.'

'Doesn't work that way,' said a new voice at the Doctor's shoulder.

It was the manservant. Chivers.

'You still here then?'

Chivers smiled. 'I'm always here, Doctor. At the side of Nathaniel Porter for the last few years. Watching over things.'

'The ever-faithful butler-manservant-person. One step behind, always in the background, never noticed. Oh, you played your part brilliantly. Well done. Question is, which one were you, and which one was he?'

Chivers smiled. 'My name is… was… 3. I was the Executive Officer aboard the *Exalted*. And I've been trapped here for many years.'

'Nathaniel Porter sussed you, didn't he?'

'Yes. Trapped me in the house – his psychic prowess kept me in his thrall. Physically, I could never leave it. If I tried, it hurt. My punishment, I suppose, because this is all my fault. I was the first of the Weave to explore. The first to contaminate both the human world and our ship.'

'Don't be stupid, of course it's not your fault. Put that nonsense out of your mind and let's focus. Now then, when Nathaniel Porter, or the Weave/Tahnn hybrid of him, needed someone to wait on him hand

216

and foot, he saw amusement in making you do that, yeah? See, not your fault.'

Chivers agreed. 'I tried to look after Oliver Marks, too. I recognised the Tahnn's handiwork on him but I was pretty useless at that. 25463 kept separating us by taking him outside into the garden.'

'And as you couldn't go out, he used Old John who was just the ticket simply because he could go outside.'

Chivers nodded. 'My crew couldn't get help. 25463 was the Tactical Officer aboard ship. He knew our defences better than anyone. He placed a sort of shield around the whole village. Humans could come and go, but we were limited.'

'I think we felt it slightly as we entered,' the Doctor said, remembering Rory's 'someone walked over my grave' moment. 'It's psychic in nature. That's why the psychic paper had no effect on him.' The Doctor eased Chivers/3 away from the bizarre partygoers. 'How long before the Glamour wears off?'

Chivers/3 shrugged. 'We have no idea how it affects a human.'

'I do.'

They turned to see a young boy, no more than 14, standing next to them. He wore thick animal skins. 'It never wears off,' he said simply.

'Who are you?' asked 3.

'I am Owain. I will be a hundred other people. Five hundred other people. Glamour has kept me alive for six thousand years.'

The Doctor looked the boy up and down, then spotted a couple of adorned leather straps around his wrist. 'Of course. Owain, modern name, John, you're Old John. Look, John, 3, we have to get out of Oliver's creation. We need to get to the Weave ship. I think I can reverse this.'

'How?'

The Doctor opened his mouth to answer but realised he couldn't. 'I honestly have no idea, but I'm brilliant at making up solutions on the spot, and frankly I've more chance of doing that at your ship, 3, than here.'

'The architecture keeps changing, Doctor,' said 3. 'I'm not sure we can get out.'

'Yes we can, I have a secret weapon. He'll be here any minute.'

'Rory?'

'Oh yes. A straightforward, simple, down-to-earth human being with no perspective on the world other than his own. He's magnificent.'

Rory was looking around the room – there had to be a way out. He'd got in, so logically there was a way out. 'You just can't see it,' he told himself. 'What would the Doctor do? He'd think laterally, Rory. So…'

He looked around. So far he'd been shown aspects of Amy Pond and a tree. So the tree… was that the answer? Was that where Amy was? Mind you, it was a pretty insignificant tree, it looked like any other tree out there.

He looked at the portraits of Amy. The triptych.

'Come on, Amy, give us a hand.'

Chapter
16

Amy Pond was awake. And she was not happy.

'Is someone going to let me out of here?' She was in a small, dark room. She could smell the damp still, so she reckoned she wasn't that far from the tree she'd been dragged through. 'Come on, bored now!'

Nothing.

Her eyes were adjusting to the dark and, after a few minutes, she realised she wasn't alone. A handful of other people were lying flat on the ground, and she reached out gingerly to touch the nearest, a rotund old lady.

Yes. She was breathing. Not dead. Not-dead people in a room – definitely a good thing. Not-sleeping people would have been better.

She tried to focus on the faces as she moved around. Tom Benson was there, a man she hadn't seen before, oh, and that was the weird manservant from the Manse.

'You lot,' she clicked her fingers. 'You lot are all duplicated back in the village, aren't you?'

The fourth and final person she found was different to the others. She wasn't just lying there, she was cocooned in a woollen, well, cocoon. Only her face was visible, and Amy held a hand near her mouth. Yup, breathing but, like the others, shallow breathing. A posh lady, nice hair, about 60. She'd seen her before... of course.

'Hello first Mrs Porter,' she said. 'Glad you're still with us and not under the patio.'

Why was Amy awake and not these others?

She'd been duplicated, too. She remembered seeing that young counsellor changing... oh. Maybe something had happened to her, and that was why Amy was awake now.

Blimey, that's what travelling with the Doctor did for you. You worked things out quickly enough, but they usually had a fairly grisly story behind them.

Amy was about to yell out again when the whole world seemed quite literally to convulse.

'Not good, Amy,' she said aloud, to comfort herself.

It was good, though. When the world stopped juddering, part of the wall opposite just melted away. Amy could actually see the walls unwrapping themselves and melting away. 'Like wool... Oh great, I'm in their ship and it's all made of wool.' She glanced back. Sure enough, Mrs Porter's wool cocoon was gone, although she wasn't waking up. Nor were any of the others.

'Still just me, then. OK.'

She stepped into another part of the ship. As she moved slowly along, she kept seeing things flicker in her peripheral vision but it wasn't till she entered a much larger area that she realised what they were.

It was the crew, unwrapping and re-knitting over and over again. Some of them were on the ground, others pressed against walls, becoming one with the walls, then emerging again, then going back in again.

No one was making a sound, but what she could glimpse of the indistinct faces suggested they weren't exactly enjoying this.

An arm reached out and grabbed her and she squealed. It was Tom Benson, she realised. Well, the woolly alien version of Tom Benson.

'I don't know what to do,' she said. 'Where's 128 or whatever she's called?'

The faux Tom Benson didn't reply, he just merged into a ship's doorway and then out again. Then in again. Then out again.

It was as if the ship was rejecting the crew... 'Like an illness. Like antibodies, kicking out a virus.'

'No, not... not a virus...' said a rasping voice at her feet.

She dropped to the floor. Pushing its way through the ground, then sinking back, then re-emerging was Commander 128.

'The ship is hurt – the Glamour… leaked out. The energy is being misused… The only way the ship can survive is by absorbing our lives. When it exhausts those, it'll die anyway.'

'OK, OK, I get that.' But 128 was gone again. 'Come on, come on,' Amy urged the woolly ground. This time a whole head popped up. 128 was really giving it all she had.

'We need the Glamour back or the ship will die.' Then she was gone again.

'Right. Find something called the Glamour – and I'm betting we're not talking a makeover – and bring it back here. Simple!'

She waited to see if 128 came back. 'I need to know how to get back to the village.'

Nothing.

Amy got back to her feet and continued walking. Something had to lead somewhere, surely…

Rory thought about what had happened when the world went mad. The two of them and limping Old John hit the deck. Oliver was in the throes of…

Where the hell were Oliver and Old John?

Old John seemed to know what was going on, so maybe he was the best bet.

'Go on,' Rory said to the picture of the tree. 'Don't show me Amy stuff, show me useful stuff.'

The tree obediently changed into a picture of a small hillock, covered with sheep.

'Great.'

He was about to suggest something else when it struck him. 'Show me a door. Out of this room, to wherever the Doctor is.'

The picture showed a wall, and Rory recognised it.

'Oh, you good scary picture thing.'

He looked around and sure enough, there was the exact bit of wall.

Closing his eyes, Rory walked at it.

Through it.

He opened his eyes to find himself at a party.

'Rory!' Someone slapped him on the shoulders. It was Oliver Marks, full of life. And possibly alcohol. 'Welcome to my new world. Free of Tahnn, free of Weave, and with my beautiful family all here.' He indicated the woman Rory had seen in the garden, plus two kids.

'Hi,' Rory said lamely. 'Don't s'pose you've spotted the Doctor. He likes a good knees-up.'

He saw Amy before Oliver could answer. He pushed his way through to her, but somehow every time he nearly got to her, she was six people away again.

'Got you!'

He was yanked away from Amy. It was the Doctor. 'It's not really her, sorry. Anyway, how did you get here? No, doesn't matter, you are here, that's the important bit. So if you are here, we can get in and out. Question is how. So yeah, actually, how did you get in here?'

'Through an invisible door.'

'Of course you did. Thank you. That's helpful.'

'No, really. It was exactly where you went out, only to me it had been sealed over with a bit of wall.'

The Doctor swung round, back and forth, back and forth. 'Focus, Doctor, focus,' he muttered. 'Think think, think. Came in through a door – what was in front of me? Paintings? No. That table? No. That huge window? Yes!' He swung around 180 degrees. 'Door's that way, Rory. Come on, you two,' he yelled to two people. Rory recognised one as Chibbers/Cheggers/whatever. The other one was a scrawny kid dressed like a Womble. The Doctor held Rory's hand, tighter than Rory thought appropriate. 'Rory, grab 3. 3, grab Owain, careful of his gammy leg.'

Gammy leg? thought Rory. *Is that Old John? Wow, some people have weird self-image problems.*

'Right,' the Doctor announced. 'Let's go. As my old friend Stitch once said, "No one gets left behind"!'

'I've seen that film,' Rory muttered to the manservant who seemed to have a number not a name. Oh. Oh he must be a Weave. 'Disney. Love a good Disney.'

Any further conversation was stopped as the Doctor ran at full pelt into what Rory hoped wasn't going to be a solid wall.

It wasn't.

They were in the hallway of the Manse.

'OK, assuming we're out of Oliver's illusion, bless him, let's get to the Weave ship.'

3 stopped. 'Doctor, there's a problem with your plan. I can't go outside.'

Rory noticed the Norfolk accent was gone, along with the subservience.

'Yeah, course you can go outside,' the Doctor said. 'Nathaniel Porter is dead. Oliver was pretty thorough in his revenge on him.'

So they exited into the night air.

'At last,' 3 murmured.

'Doctor,' said Rory. 'If all that in the Manse is an illusion, what's going to happen to Oliver when it stops?'

'If it stops,' said 3.

'When it stops,' confirmed the Doctor. 'And Rory, I don't know. Much as I like Oliver and feel sorry for him, right now, getting the Glamour back aboard that ship is more important.'

'Why?'

'Because it doesn't belong on Earth. Look at Oliver. Look at what he's done with it. Imagine if it spread and everyone's fantasies came to life. Blimey, imagine your fantasies brought to life. That's a scary thought. Poor old Amy wouldn't know what'd hit her.'

Rory frowned but chose to say nothing.

They ran as fast as they could to the schoolyard, Owain/Old John having stopped and told them to go on without him – his leg was killing him.

The Doctor reached the entrance to the dig first and bolted down it. By the time Rory and 3 caught up, he was staring at the exposed side of the *Exalted*, a massive tear in it. Standing next to it, unmoving, like freeze-frames on a DVD, were Enola Porter and her team.

'OK, so we can see what happened here.' The Doctor pointed behind him, to Marten Heinke. '3, see if you can free your chum there.'

'I daren't.'

'Why not?'

'Same reason I'm staying in my human disguise. If we lose concentration, we'll be absorbed by the ship as it tries to regain energy.'

'3, don't see if you can free your chum there, instead, tell me how we get the Glamour away from Olly and back into your ship.'

'I have absolutely no idea.'

'Great. Fabulous. Absolutely marvellous.'

'Couldn't we just…'

'What, Rory, what? Couldn't we just what?'

'Doesn't matter, daft idea.'

'Daft ideas I like. Right now I could do with a daft idea. I prefer great ideas, but daft will do.'

'Couldn't we tempt it back. I mean, it presumably went to Oliver because his need to create a fake world was greater than Nathaniel Porter's.'

The Doctor said nothing.

'Ah well.'

The Doctor walked over to Enola Porter, waved a hand in front of her. No reaction. 'She's no good to us, then. Your idea is brilliant, Rory. But I'm not sure how we can make it work.'

'About blooming time!'

Amy Pond was stepping out of the rent in the ship. She hugged the Doctor and then Rory, who noted happily that he got the longer hug.

'Doctor,' she said, 'we have to help Commander 128 and her crew. The ship's absorbing them.'

'Back ten seconds, already giving orders. Yup, this is the real Amelia Pond all right. But she's right, 3.'

'Oooh, I saw your original inside there.' Amy waved at the ship's interior.

The Doctor clicked his fingers. '3. You can't manipulate the Glamour, can you?'

'Of course I can.'

'Yes, all right, but not in your current state. Otherwise, why did it go for Oliver? Why not any of the actual crew – I assume it's actually programmed to work for you lot. Entertainment system on long voyages, that sort of thing, yes?'

'Yes. But no, it doesn't work on injured crewmembers. An illness, a fever, the Glamour could go utterly haywire.'

'Rather like it has done with Olly. So it can't go to a damaged Weave mind – and you're all damaged anyway in your natural state *because* the Glamour can't go to you – oh, God bless Oroboros-esque problems.'

'You what?'

'Catch 22, Rory. To stop the Glamour we need an undamaged Weave body to draw it out. All the Weave bodies are damaged by the Glamour, and the only way to un-damage them is to use the Glamour, which we can't…'

'Because all their bodies are damaged, got it.'

'So we need something more damaged than Oliver's mind. Or at least a confused one. You, me, Amy, old limpy John, wherever he is, we're useless. We're all too self-aware right now. But if one of the sleeping humans in there were suddenly awoken…'

'No good, Doctor,' said 3. 'Whenever we take a human form, we are obliged to give them full disclosure first. They all knew what was happening to them.'

'That's true,' said Amy. 'I did.'

'So in there is the real Chivers, hopefully the real Marten Heinke and the real Nancy Thirman. That's all of you, yes, 3?'

'Mrs Porter!' shouted Amy.

'She's over there Amy,' the Doctor pointed at Enola.

'Oh not her. The *first* Mrs Porter.'

'Dead,' said 3.

'No, she's not. She's asleep in there. With the rest

of them. She was in a cocoony thing, not like us. First-class service, I suppose, for the local aristocracy.'

'No.' 3 grabbed the Doctor. 'If Amy's right...'

'She's always right,' Rory muttered.

'If she was in a cocoon, it's because she's in hibernation. She's not been copied, she's being fed nutrients from the ship. There's no copy of Mrs Porter, so she won't have been conditioned. Most likely 25463 tried to kill her and my people found her and saved her life.'

The Doctor grinned. 'Wake her up, she'll have the biggest shock, show her an alien and BAM! The Glamour will come straight to her like a shot. The mixture of confused mind and its own ship, best bait we've got.'

Rory frowned. 'But you're only guessing all this, aren't you?'

'Course I am,' said the Doctor. 'It's more fun that way.' He ran into the ship, followed by the others.

Amy led the way back to the chamber. It took a while.

'Blimey,' the Doctor said. 'This ship's huge.'

'It stretches right out of the village and under—'

'A huge tree,' Rory finished Amy's sentence. 'So that's what that was all about.'

'What what was all about?'

'I asked a magic picture to tell me where you were, and it showed me a tree.'

'Magic picture?'

'Oh, clever ship,' the Doctor stroked the hull. 'You grew all the way under Nathaniel Porter's psychic cage so the Weave could get in and out.' He clapped his hands. 'Right, let's wake these people up.'

3 reached out with his hand, and it started stretching into wool. 'This is dangerous, Doctor, because if I go too far into my true form, the ship will absorb me.'

The Doctor looked at him. 'You know how you told me this was all your fault, and I said not to be stupid, that it wasn't?'

'Yes.'

'Well I lied. It was *entirely* your fault so, frankly, it's up to you to put it right.'

3 looked at him, and slowly nodded. His woollen form extended, brushing each of the sleeping forms. Almost instantly, they started to come round.

The Doctor turned to Amy and Rory. 'Get them out of here. Back to somewhere that isn't the Manse, but far away from here.'

'Why?'

'Because if this goes to plan, I'll need this ship to take off pretty quickly. And when it does, it'll take the school, these woods and anything else above the ship with it.'

Rory and Amy started herding the rather confused and woozy Nancy Thirman, Chivers, Marten Heinke and Tom Benson away as fast as possible. 'See you up there,' the Doctor yelled at them.

After they'd gone, he turned back to 3. 'This is going to hurt you a lot, isn't it?'

'The ship will try to reabsorb me if I go any further into my own body. But I need to, to wake her up.'

'I need more of you than that. She needs to see you do it, see you get reabsorbed. Because I need this poor old woman to be utterly terrified, shocked. Sorry.'

3 smiled. 'I know you are.'

And he instantly became Weave, spreading his woollen hands around Mrs Porter's head.

She woke with a start and was about to speak when 3 gave a terrible scream as he was savagely drawn back into the wall of the ship.

As he vanished, Mrs Porter, like any well-bred lady from the rural 1930s just said: 'Young man, kindly tell me what on earth is going on.'

The Doctor stared. 'What? No! Be scared, woman! Shocked! Amazed! Terrified! Anything! Why aren't you scared?'

'Of what?'

'Oh, blimey, that British stiff upper lip. Well, that was a waste of 3's sacrifice.'

Amy and Rory were helping their three charges stumble through the ship. When they finally reached the rent in the side of the ship, the real Marten Heinke saw the fake Marten Heinke. He punched him.

And the tableau was broken, as the fake Heinke became Weave historian 41200 and was immediately reabsorbed by the hull of the ship before anyone could speak.

Enola Porter and her team woke up, too, including Walpole Spune, who saw the Weave Heinke vanish and let out a long, terrified scream of fear.

Oliver Marks was kissing his lovely wife Daisy when she vanished. When the whole party vanished. When the Glamour vanished, leaving him alone in the now empty Manse.

And he remembered everything.

Chapter
17

As the Glamour returned to the ship, the effect was instantaneous. It briefly hovered by Walpole Spune's shaking body for a second but then, as if deciding between his cowardly mind and its natural habitat, it spread itself back into the walls of the ship itself and, within just a few moments, the crew started to re-emerge.

Alive. Well. Safe. And that meant the threat was all over.

Five minutes later, Commander 128, Executive Officer 3 and the rest of the crew were facing the Doctor on the now reassembled bridge.

Enola Porter and her archaeology team were staring in amazement. So were Nancy Thirman, Chivers and Tom Benson.

The Doctor pulled Amy aside. 'I thought I said get them away from here?'

'The ship hasn't taken off yet.'

'OK, so I may have misjudged that bit, it took longer to put the ship back together now the Glamour has been reabsorbed.' The Doctor looked over to 128. 'By the way, Commander, I can see why the Tahnn wanted it. You think it's a gorgeous high-def 3D cinema, but they saw its potential as a weapon. Remember that when you get home.'

128 smiled sadly. 'I'm not sure we can get home. The ship can't fly. We have lost three of my crew. In a normal battle scenario, the ship has enough energy to limp home. But taking off from here, with the thrust it'll need to get us out from underground, without my full complement, it's impossible.'

'I'm not famous, am I, Doctor?' Enola Porter stepped forward. 'In the future I mean?'

'As non-sequiturs go, that's a good one, Enola. But no, no, you're not, sorry.'

'And I know why.'

'Why?'

'I discovered an alien spaceship. I mean, I should be renowned. But I'm not, which means either I die quite soon after leaving Shalford Heights or something else equally ghastly happens.'

'And your point is?'

'Commander, my name is Enola Porter. I'm an adventuress, explorer and investigator. I know I'm only a human, but if it would help, I'm sure I can operate some switches or levers. Would my presence aboard your starship help?'

'Probably not,' intervened the Doctor. 'I think you have to be at one with the ship. Made of wool-stuff.'

'Oh.' Enola looked downcast. 'It was worth a try.'

128 shrugged. 'It *is* worth a try actually. If it fails, you haven't lost anything. If it succeeds...'

'Now hang on,' the Doctor started, but Enola cut him off.

'Thank you, Commander. I would be honoured.' She looked at her band of archaeologists. 'The other Marten, he told me of wonders, of dreams out there, amongst the stars. And these people need help. Anyone else game?'

Walpole Spune shook his head. 'Madness, woman, utter madness.'

Christopher Maginn smiled sadly. 'It sounds a great lark, Enola, but no, not me.'

Hamish Ridley and the real Marten Heinke shared a look. Heinke wandered over to Maginn and Walpole. 'Nein.'

But Ridley was looking around the ship. 'Yeah, why not. Customs can't reach me up there in the stars, can they?'

'This is madness,' the Doctor muttered. 'You'll never get back. You'll never see Earth again.'

'Are you sure none of you will join us?' 3 asked the archaeologists. 'We still need someone to replace 6011.'

'That'll be me, then.' Oliver Marks walked up to the Commander and saluted her. 'If you'll have me, Commander.'

'Olly,' the Doctor nudged him. 'Are you sure?'

'I had a taste of a world with Daisy in, Doctor. It was bloody marvellous, while it lasted, but it wasn't real. I can't ever have my old life back. This? This is an opportunity.'

The Doctor, Amy and Rory looked around the bridge of the *Exalted*.

'Goodbye and good luck,' the Doctor said and turned and walked away, the other humans following him.

He led them out of the dig tunnel, and away from the school, swiftly catching Nancy Thirman's arm as she tried to get back to her library.

'But my books…'

'Are going to go *poof!* in about two minutes, Miss Thirman. Possessions aren't worth a life.'

They walked back towards the Manse where the first Mrs Porter and Old John, who was clearly his old, old self again, stood watching. Ever the good servant, despite his long absence, Chivers quickly escorted his mistress into the Manse, while the others stood and watched and waited.

And then, with a sufficiently loud bang, the school vanished completely, taking most of the grounds with it as the Weave ship successfully roared away from Earth and out into space.

'It worked,' Rory said.

'I didn't expect it to, I have to say,' the Doctor grinned. 'Nice to know there are still a few surprises left in the universe.'

They all stood outside the Manse, looking down the road towards the crater where the school had once stood.

'Wow,' said Amy. 'That's a big hole.'

Rory laughed but stopped as they heard a cry from the Manse behind them.

As the group turned, they saw Nancy Thirman was on the ground, Old John collapsed before her, his head resting in her lap, looking up at her.

A tear ran down his cheek as they came over.

'I'm sorry, Doctor,' he said. 'So sorry. I can't move.'

'I half-expected to see you at the ship, with Olly,' the Doctor smiled. 'You could have seen what you held guardianship over for all these years.'

'And meet my Gods? Face to face. No. No, thank you.'

'Not Gods, John. Just people. Like you and me.'

'One thing I have learned in my long life, Doctor. Never meet your heroes or gods. They often turn out to have feet of clay.'

'Or,' Amy smiled at him, 'in this case, feet of wool.'

'John,' the Doctor said, taking his hand as he knelt down. 'John, by being guardian to that ship, you helped saved us all. The people of Shalford Heights have their lives back. And being Great and British, they'll soon get over this. Forget it ever happened. Rewrite their personal history, claim it was all a bad dream or a collective hallucination. Or something. Whatever. But the important thing is, we all owe our lives in no small part to you.'

Old John smiled. 'Six thousand or so years, and finally, it's over. They've gone home at last.'

'And you protected them so well all that time,' said Rory.

The Doctor smiled. 'I envy you all that knowledge you accumulated over the centuries. And I admire the secrets that you've kept.'

'You'll be fine,' Amy added, but Old John's body convulsed. She looked at the Doctor.

'The Weave ship is leaving our atmosphere,' he said.

'And without it, so goes the magic. The Sky Gods are taking back their magic.'

'Now, John, I told you – they're not gods.' The Doctor stroked his hair, gently.

Old John laughed then coughed. 'Ah, but I choose not to agree, Doctor. They were *my* gods. They gave me life, purpose. Immortality even. And they thanked me. As they took off on their new journey, I heard them.' Old John smiled at that. 'They said, "Thank you, Owain, son of Wulf".'

And he was dead, the smile still on his lips.

Chapter
18

No one said very much till they were a few metres from the TARDIS, in the sheep field where they'd first landed.

'Rory.' The Doctor stopped suddenly. 'What's up?'

'Is that it, Doctor? We came here, something huge happened, people died, people lost their homes, everything they believed in. And we just walk away? Is that how it goes?'

The Doctor fiddled with his bow tie, a sure sign he was feeling awkward. 'It's how life, the universe works, Rory. If we stayed behind after everything we do, we could end up spending days, weeks, years trying to help one community, one world rebuild. But I have to move on, otherwise another world might fall under the oppressors. We've done all we can here. We need to go.'

Rory nodded. He understood. 'Yeah I know. There's nothing we can do to bring them back.' He sighed. 'I'm also thinking about Oliver Marks and what post-traumatic stress disorder did to him, and how back in 2010 I could at least give people like him some understanding. There are people stuck here in 1936, after everything that's happened, who will suffer in silence for years. Unable to understand what is wrong with them. Every time they hear a loud bang, or feel a tremor, or hear something in the sky. Or see a ball of wretched knitting wool.'

The Doctor interrupted and hugged Rory very, very tightly indeed, then kissed him on the forehead. 'Keep that in your head, Rory. Always. I need that compassion, that point of view around me. Because sometimes I forget that I've been doing all this for so long, that there are consequences.' He pulled away, leaving Rory rather stunned at this public display of affection.

The Doctor looked at Amy. 'He's a keeper, this one.'

'I know,' Amy said. 'That's why I'm marrying him in about seventy-five years' time.'

The Doctor smiled at his two companions. Then stopped. 'Blimey, this is all a bit touchy-feely isn't it?' He clapped his hands together. 'Come on, TARDIS time, quick bath and then on to Rio.'

'Rio? Yeah, right,' said Amy. 'Like that's ever

gonna happen.'

'Oh ye of little faith,' said the Doctor and promptly vanished from sight.

Rory and Amy scurried over and realised he'd fallen down the same hillock and landed in the same sheep dip.

Baaaa said a sheep.

'Oh, shut up,' said the Doctor crossly.

Rory cracked a smile and then suddenly kissed Amy on the lips. After a moment he started to break away, but she pulled him closer for a few more seconds, then broke away herself.

'What was that for?'

He shrugged. 'Cos I love you. Cos despite what I just said, I do love all this stuff with him-in-the-sheep-dip down there.'

'Well,' said Amy. 'Let's stick at it for a bit longer. And then we can spend the rest of our lives together, with all these memories, good and bad.'

Rory grinned. 'I like that idea. I like it a lot. Building memories together. Brilliant.'

A bedraggled, wet, smelly Doctor hauled himself up to the TARDIS, opened the door and stomped in.

'And that,' Amy said as they followed him in, 'is a sight neither of us will ever forget.'

Seconds later, a flock of startled sheep began to run away, as the TARDIS noisily and windily left Norfolk behind and went somewhere else entirely.

Acknowledgements

Special thanks to Justin, Steve and Lee for their patience.

To Oli, David, Brian and Una for being inspirational.

To Scott, Phil, Eòghann and Tony for the essential road trips.

To Shaun, Robbie and everyone for further inspiration at Gallifrey One.

Most of all, to Mark for the important, frank and honest discussions about PTSD. Oh and a fab swimming pool!

Available now from BBC Books:

DOCTOR WHO

Apollo 23

by Justin Richards

£6.99 ISBN 978 1 846 07200 0

An astronaut in full spacesuit appears out of thin air in a busy shopping centre. Maybe it's a publicity stunt.

A photo shows a well-dressed woman in a red coat lying dead at the edge of a crater on the dark side of the moon – beside her beloved dog 'Poochie'. Maybe it's a hoax.

But, as the Doctor and Amy find out, these are just minor events in a sinister plan to take over every human being on Earth. The plot centres on a secret military base on the moon – that's where Amy and the TARDIS are.

The Doctor is back on Earth, and without the TARDIS there's no way he can get to the moon to save Amy and defeat the aliens.

Or is there? The Doctor discovers one last great secret that could save humanity: Apollo 23.

A thrilling, all-new adventure featuring the Doctor and Amy, as played by Matt Smith and Karen Gillan in the spectacular hit series from BBC Television.

DOCTOR █ WHO
Night of the Humans

by David Llewellyn

£6.99 ISBN 978 1 846 07969 6

250,000 years' worth of junk floating in deep space, home to the shipwrecked Sittuun, the carnivorous Sollogs, and worst of all – the Humans.

The Doctor and Amy arrive on this terrifying world in the middle of an all-out frontier war between Sittuun and Humans, and the countdown has already started. There's a comet in the sky, and it's on a collision course with the Gyre…

When the Doctor is kidnapped, it's up to Amy and 'galaxy-famous swashbuckler' Dirk Slipstream to save the day.

But who is Slipstream, exactly? And what is he really doing here?

A thrilling, all-new adventure featuring the Doctor and Amy, as played by Matt Smith and Karen Gillan in the spectacular hit series from BBC Television.

DOCTOR █ WHO
Nuclear Time
by Oli Smith

£6.99 ISBN 978 1 846 07989 4

Colorado, 1981. The Doctor, Amy and Rory arrive in Appletown – an idyllic village in the remote American desert where the townsfolk go peacefully about their suburban routines. But when two more strangers arrive, things begin to change.

The first is a mad scientist – whose warnings are cut short by an untimely and brutal death. The second is the Doctor…

As death falls from the sky, the Doctor is trapped. The TARDIS is damaged, and the Doctor finds he is living backwards through time. With Amy and Rory being hunted through the suburban streets of the Doctor's own future and getting farther away with every passing second, he must unravel the secrets of Appletown before time runs out…

A thrilling, all-new adventure featuring the Doctor, Amy and Rory, as played by Matt Smith, Karen Gillan and Arthur Darvill in the spectacular hit series from BBC Television.